Jack Kerouac was born in 1922 of a French-Canadian family in the factory town of Lowell, Massachusetts, and died in 1969 in St. Petersburg, Florida, where he had gone to live a year before with his third wife and invalid mother. He spent his childhood in Lowell and his early adulthood in the East, attending Columbia College in New York. Later he sailed to various Atlantic and Mediterranean ports as a merchant seaman, and rambled, as his books suggest over much of North America. His first book, *The Town and the City,* was published in 1950. Then unable to find a publisher for *On the Road* in 1951, he spent six years "writing whatever came into my head, hopping freights, hitch-hiking, and working as a railroad brakeman, deckhand and scullion on merchant ships, government fire lookout, and hundreds of assorted jobs." *On the Road* was published in 1957 and it brought him immediate fame and acclaim. His other books came in quick succession and were translated into eighteen languages. He has imprinted himself on modern American literature as the father and authentic voice of the "beat generation." His books include *Visions of Neal, Doctor Sax, The Subterraneans, Springtime Mary, Lonesome Traveler, San Francisco Blues, Dharma Bums, Book of Dreams, Wake Up, Mexico City Blues, Visions of Gerard, Satori in Paris, Scripture of Golden Eternity, Vanity of Duluoz,* and *Pic.*

THE
SUBTERRANEANS

Jack Kerouac

BALLANTINE BOOKS • NEW YORK

BALLANTINE BOOKS
A Division of Random House, Inc.

THE
SUBTERRANEANS

ONCE I was young and had so much more orientation and could talk with nervous intelligence about everything and with clarity and without as much literary preambling as this; in other words this is the story of an unself-confident man, at the same time of an egomaniac, naturally, facetious won't do—just to start at the beginning and let the truth seep out,

that's what I'll do—. It began on a warm summernight—
ah, she was sitting on a fender with Julien Alexander
who is . . . let me begin with the history of the subterraneans of San Francisco . . .

Julien Alexander is the angel of the subterraneans,
the subterraneans is a name invented by Adam Moorad
who is a poet and friend of mine who said "They are
hip without being slick, they are intelligent without
being corny, they are intellectual as hell and know all
about Pound without being pretentious or talking too
much about it, they are very quiet, they are very Christlike." Julien certainly is Christlike. I was coming down
the street with Larry O'Hara old drinking buddy of
mine from all the times in San Francisco in my long
and nervous and mad careers I've gotten drunk and
in fact cadged drinks off friends with such "genial"
regularity nobody really cared to notice or announce
that I am developing or was developing, in my youth,
such bad freeloading habits though of course they did
notice but liked me and as Sam said "Everybody comes
to you for your gasoline boy, that's some filling station
you got there" or say words to that effect—old Larry
O'Hara always nice to me, a crazy Irish young business-
man of San Francisco with Balzacian backroom in his
bookstore where they'd smoke tea and talk of the old
days of the great Basie band or the days of the great
Chu Berry—of whom more anon since she got involved
with him too as she had to get involved with everyone

because of knowing me who am nervous and many
leveled and not in the least one-souled—not a piece
of my pain has showed yet—or suffering—Angels, bear
with me—I'm not even looking at the page but straight
ahead into the sadglint of my wallroom and at a Sarah
Vaughan Gerry Mulligan Radio KROW show on the
desk in the form of a radio, in other words, they were
sitting on the fender of a car in front of the Black Mask
bar on Montgomery Street, Julien Alexander the Christlike unshaved thin youthful quiet strange almost as you
or as Adam might say apocalyptic angel or saint of the
subterraneans, certainly star (now), and she, Mardou
Fox, whose face when first I saw it in Dante's bar around
the corner made me think, "By God, I've got to get
involved with that little woman" and maybe too because
she was Negro. Also she had the same face that Rita
Savage a girlhood girlfriend of my sister's had, and
of whom among other things I used to have daydreams
of her between my legs while kneeling on the floor of
the toilet, I on the seat, with her special cool lips and
Indian-like hard high soft cheekbones—same face, but
dark, sweet, with little eyes honest glittering and intense
she Mardou was leaning saying something extremely
earnestly to Ross Wallenstein (Julien's friend) leaning
over the table, deep—"I got to get involved with her"—
I tried to shoot her the glad eye the sex eye she never
had a notion of looking up or seeing—I must explain,
I'd just come off a ship in New York, paid off before the

[3]

trip to Kobe Japan because of trouble with the steward and my inability to be gracious and in fact human and like an ordinary guy while performing my chores as saloon messman (and you must admit now I'm sticking to the facts), a thing typical of me, I would treat the first engineer and the other officers with backwards-falling politeness, it finally drove them angry, they wanted me to say something, maybe gruff, in the morning, while setting their coffee down and instead of which silently on crepefeet I rushed to do their bidding and never cracked a smile or if so a sick one, a superior one, all having to do with that loneliness angel riding on my shoulder as I came down warm Montgomery Street that night and saw Mardou on the fender with Julien, remembering, "O there's the girl I gotta get involved with, I wonder if she's going with any of these boys"—dark, you could barely see her in the dim street—her feet in thongs of sandals of such sexuality-looking greatness I wanted to kiss her, them—having no notion of anything though.

The subterraneans were hanging outside the Mask in the warm night, Julien on the fender, Ross Wallenstein standing up, Roger Beloit the great bop tenorman, Walt Fitzpatrick who was the son of a famous director and had grown up in Hollywood in an atmosphere of Greta Garbo parties at dawn and Chaplin falling in the door drunk, several other girls, Harriet the ex-wife of Ross Wallenstein a kind of blonde with soft expressionless features and wearing a simple almost housewife-in-the-kitchen cotton dress but softly bellysweet to look at—as another confession must be made, as many I must make ere time's sup—I am crudely malely sexual and cannot help myself and have lecherous and so on propensities as almost all my male readers no doubt are the same—confession after confession, I am a Canuck, I could not speak English till I was 5 or 6, at 16 I spoke with a halting accent and was a big blue baby in school though varsity basketball later and if not for that no one would have noticed I could cope in any way with the world (underself-confidence) and would have been put in the madhouse for some kind of inadequacy—

But now let me tell Mardou herself (difficult to make a real confession and show what happened when you're such an egomaniac all you can do is to take off on big paragraphs about minor details about yourself and the big soul details about others go sitting and waiting around)—in any case, therefore, also there was Fritz Nicholas the titular leader of the subterraneans, to whom I said (having met him New Year's Eve in a Nob Hill swank apartment sitting cross-legged like a peyote Indian on a thick rug wearing a kind of clean white Russian shirt and a crazy Isadora Duncan girl with long blue hair on his shoulder smoking pot and talking about Pound and peyote) (thin also Christlike with a faun's look and young and serious and like the father of the group, as say, suddenly you'd see him in the Black

Mask sitting there with head thrown back thin dark eyes watching everybody as if in sudden slow astonishment and "Here we are little ones and now what my dears," but also a great dope man, anything in the form of kicks he would want at any time and very intense) I said to him, "Do you know this girl, the dark one?"— "Mardou?"—"That her name? Who she go with?"—"No one in particular just now, this has been an incestuous group in its time," a very strange thing he said to me there, as we walked to his old beat 36 Chevvy with no backseat parked across from the bar for the purpose of picking up some tea for the group to get all together, as, I told Larry, "Man, let's get some tea."—"And what for you want all those people?"—"I want to dig them as a group," saying this, too, in front of Nicholas so perhaps he might appreciate my sensitivity being a stranger to the group and yet immediately, etc., perceiving their value—facts, facts, sweet philosophy long deserted me with the juices of other years fled—incestuous—there was another final great figure in the group who was however now this summer not here but in Paris, Jack Steen, very interesting Leslie Howard-like little guy who walked (as Mardou later imitated for me) like a Viennese philosopher with soft arms swinging slight side flow and long slow flowing strides, coming to a stop on corner with imperious soft pose—he too had had to do with Mardou and as I learned later most weirdly—but now my first crumb of information concerning this girl I was

SEEKING to get involved with as if not enough trouble already or other old romances hadn't taught me that message of pain, keep asking for it, for like—

Out of the bar were pouring interesting people, the night making a great impression on me, some kind of Truman Capote-haired dark Marlon Brando with a beautiful thin birl or girl in boy slacks with stars in her eyes and hips that seemed so soft when she put her hands in her slacks I could see the change—and dark thin slackpant legs dropping down to little feet, and that face, and with them a guy with another beautiful doll, the guy's name Rob and he's some kind of adventurous Israeli soldier with a British accent whom I suppose you might find in some Riviera bar at 5 A.M. drinking everything in sight alphabetically with a bunch of interesting crazy international-set friends on a spree—Larry O'Hara introducing me to Roger Beloit (I did not believe that this young man with ordinary face in front of me was that great poet I'd revered in my youth, my youth, my youth, that is, 1948, I keep saying my youth)—"This is Roger Beloit?—I'm Bennett Fitzpatrick" (Walt's father) which brought a smile to Roger Beloit's face—Adam Moorad by now having emerged from the night was also there and the night would open—

So we all did go to Larry's and Julien sat on the floor in front of an open newspaper in which was the tea (poor quality L.A. but good enough) and rolled, or "twisted," as Jack Steen, the absent one, had said to me the previous New Year's and that having been my first contact with the subterraneans, he'd asked to roll a stick for me and I'd said really coldly "What for? I roll my own" and immediately the cloud crossed his sensitive little face, etc., and he hated me—and so cut me all the night when he had a chance—but now Julien was on the floor, cross-legged, and himself now twisting for the group and everybody droned the conversations which I certainly won't repeat, except, it was, like, "I'm looking at this book by Percepied—who's Percepied, has he been busted yet?" and such small talk, or, while listening to Stan Kenton talking about the music of tomorrow and we hear a new young tenorman come on, Ricci Comucca, Roger Beloit says, moving back expressive thin purple lips, "This is the music of tomorrow?" and Larry O'Hara telling his usual stock repertoire anecdotes. In the 36 Chevvy on the way, Julien, sitting beside me on the floor, had stuck out his hand and said, "My name's Julien Alexander, I have something, I conquered Egypt," and then Mardou stuck her hand out to Adam Moorad and introduced herself, saying, "Mardou Fox," but didn't think of doing it to me which should have been my first inkling of the prophecy of what was to come, so I had to stick my hand at her and say, "Leo Percepied my name" and shake—ah, you always go for the ones who don't really want you—she really wanted Adam Moorad, she had just been rejected coldly and subterraneanly by Julien—she was interested in thin ascetic strange intellectuals of San Francisco and Berkeley and not in big paranoiac bums of ships and railroads and novels and all that hatefulness which in myself is to myself so evident and so to others too—though and because ten years younger than I seeing none of my virtues which anyway had long been drowned under years of drugtaking and desiring to die, to give up, to give it all up and forget it all, to die in the dark star—it was I stuck out my hand, not she—ah time.

But in eyeing her little charms I only had the foremost one idea that I had to immerse my lonely being ("A big sad lonely man," is what she said to me one night later, seeing me suddenly in the chair) in the warm bath and salvation of her thighs—the intimacies of young-lovers in a bed, high, facing eye to eye, breast to breast naked, organ to organ, knee to shivering goose-pimpled knee, exchanging existential and loveracts for a crack at making it—"making it" the big expression with her, I can see the little out-pushing teeth through the little redlips seeing "making it"—the key to pain—she sat in the corner, by the window, she was being "separated" or "aloof" or "prepared to cut out from this group" for her own reasons.—In the corner I went, not leaning my head on her but on the wall and tried silent communication, then quiet words (as befit party) and North Beach words, "What are you reading?" and for the first time she opened her mouth and spoke to me communicating a full thought and my heart didn't exactly sink but wondered when I heard the cultured funny tones of part Beach, part I. Magnin model, part Berkeley, part Negro highclass, something, a mixture of *langue* and style of talking and use of words I'd never heard before except in certain rare girls of course *white* and so strange even Adam at once noticed and commented with me that night—but definitely the new bop generation way of speaking, you don't say *I*, you say "ahy" or "Oy" and long ways, like oft or erstwhile "effeminate" way of speaking so when you hear it in men at first it has a disagreeable sound and when you hear it in women it's charming but much too strange, and a sound I had already definitely and wonderingly heard in the voice of new bop singers like Jerry Winters especially with Kenton band on the record *Yes Daddy Yes* and maybe in Jeri Southern too— but my heart sank for the Beach has always hated me, cast me out, overlooked me, shat on me, from the beginning in 1943 on in—for look, coming down the street I am some kind of hoodlum and then when they learn I'm not a hoodlum but some kind of crazy saint they don't like it and moreover they're afraid I'll suddenly become a hoodlum anyway and slug them and break things and this I have almost done anyway and in my adolescence did so, as one time I roamed through North Beach with the Stanford basketball team, specifically with Red Kelly whose wife (rightly?) died in Redwood City in 1946, the whole team behind us, the Garetta brothers besides, he pushed a violinist a queer into a doorway and I pushed another one in, he slugged his, I glared at mine, I was 18, I was a nannybeater and fresh as a daisy too—now, seeing this past in the scowl and glare and horror and the beat of my brow-pride they wanted nothing to do with me, and so I of course also knew that Mardou had real genuine distrust and dislike of me as I sat there "trying to (not make IT) but make her"—unhiplike, brash, smiling, the false hysterical "compulsive" smiling they call it—me hot—them cool— and also I had on a very noxious unbeachlike shirt, bought on Broadway in New York when I thought I'd be cutting down the gangplanks in Kobe, a foolish Crosby Hawaiian shirt with designs, which malelike and vain after the original honest humilities of my regular self (really) with the smoking of two drags of tea I felt constrained to open an extra button down and so show my tanned, hairy chest—which must have disgusted her—in any case she didn't look, and spoke little and low—and was intent on Julien who was squatting with his back to her—and she listened and murmured the laughter in the general talk—most of the talk being conducted by O'Hara and loudspeaking Roger Beloit and that intelligent adventurous Rob and I, too silent, listening, digging, but in the tea vanity occasionally throwing in "perfect" (I thought) remarks which were "too perfect" but to Adam Moorad who'd known me all the time clear indication of my awe and listening and respect of the group in fact, and to them this new

person throwing in remarks intended to sow his hipness—
all horrible, and unredeemable.—Although at first, before
the puffs, which were passed around Indian style, I had
the definite sensation of being able to come close with
Mardou and involved and making her that very first
night, that is taking off with her alone if only for coffee
but with the puffs which made me pray reverently and
in serious secrecy for the return of my pre-puff "sanity"
I became extremely unself-confident, overtrying, positive
she didn't like me, hating the facts—remembering now
the first night I met my Nicki Peters love in 1948 in
Adam Moorad's pad in (then) the Fillmore, I was
standing unconcerned and beerdrinking in the kitchen
as ever (and at home working furiously on a huge novel,
mad, cracked, confident, young, talented as never since)
when she pointed to my profile shadow on the pale
green wall and said, "How beautiful your profile is,"
which so nonplussed me and (like the tea) made me
unself-confident, attentive, attempting to "begin to make
her," to act in that way which by her almost hypnotic
suggestion now led to the first preliminary probings
into pride vs. pride and beauty or beatitude or sensitivity
versus the stupid neurotic nervousness of the phallic
type, forever conscious of his phallus, his tower, of
women as wells—the truth of the matter being there,
but the man unhinged, unrelaxed, and now it is no longer
1948 but 1953 with cool generations and I five years
older, or younger, having to make it (or make the

women) with a new style and stow the nervousness—
in any case, I gave up consciously trying to make Mardou
and settled down to a night of digging the great new
perplexing group of subterraneans Adam had discovered
and named on the Beach.

But from the first Mardou was indeed self-dependent
and independent announcing she wanted no one, nothing to do with anyone, ending (after me) with same—
which now in the cold unblessing night I feel in the air,
this announcement of hers, and that her little teeth are
no longer mine but probably my enemy's lapping at
them and giving her the sadistic treatment she probably
loves as I had given her none—murders in the air—and
that bleak corner where a lamp shines, and winds
swirl, a paper, fog, I see the great discouraged face of
myself and my so-called love drooping in the lane, no
good—as before it had been melancholy droopings in
hot chairs, downcast by moons (though tonight's the
great night of the harvest moon)— as where then, before, it was the recognition of the need for my return
to world-wide love as a great writer should do, like a
Luther, a Wagner, now this warm thought of greatness
is a big chill in the wind—for greatness dies too—ah
and who said I was great—and supposing one were a
great writer, a secret Shakespeare of the pillow night?
or really so—a Baudelaire's poem is not worth his grief—
his grief—(It was Mardou finally said to me, "I would
have preferred the happy man to the unhappy poems

he's left us," which I agree with and I am Baudelaire, and love my brown mistress and I too leaned to her belly and listened to the rumbling underground)—but I should have known from her original announcement of independence to believe in the sincerity of her distaste for involvement, instead hurling on at her as if and because in fact I wanted to be hurt and "lacerate" myself—one more laceration yet and they'll pull the blue sod on, and make my box plop boy—for now death bends big wings over my window, I see it, I hear it, I smell it, I see it in the limp hang of my shirts destined to be not worn, new-old, stylish-out-of-date, neckties snakelike behung I don't even use any more, new blankets for autumn peace beds now writhing rushing cots on the sea of self-murder—loss—hate—paranoia—it was her little face I wanted to enter, and did—

That morning when the party was at its pitch I was in Larry's bedroom again admiring the red light and remembering the night we'd had Mickey in there the three of us, Adam and Larry and myself, and had benny and a big sexball amazing to describe in itself—when Larry ran in and said, "Man you gonna make it with her tonight?"—"I'd shore like to—I dunno—."—"Well man find out, ain't much time left, whatsamatter with you, we bring all these people to the house and give em all that tea and now all my beer from the icebox, man we gotta get something out of it, work on it—" "Oh, you like her?"—"I like anybody as far as that goes man—but I

mean, after all." Which led me to a short unwillful
abortive fresh effort, some look, glance, remark, sitting
next to her in corner, I gave up and at dawn she cut
out with the others who all went for coffee and I went
down there with Adam to see her again (following the
group down the stairs five minutes later) and they were
there but she wasn't, independently darkly brooding,
she'd gone off to her stuffy little place in Heavenly
Lane on Telegraph Hill.

So I went home and for several days in sexual phantasies it was she, her dark feet, thongs of sandals, dark
eyes, little soft brown face, Rita Savage-like cheeks and
lips, little secretive intimacy and somehow now softly
snakelike charm as befits a little thin brown woman
disposed to wearing dark clothes, poor beat subterranean
clothes. . . .

A few nights later Adam with an evil smile announced
he had run into her in a Third Street bus and they'd
gone to his place to talk and drink and had a big long
talk which Leroy-like culminated in Adam sitting naked
reading Chinese poetry and passing the stick and ending
up laying in the bed. "And she's very affectionate, God,
the way suddenly she wraps her arms around you as
if for no other reason but pure sudden affection."—"Are
you going to make it? have an affair with her?"—"Well
now let me—actually I tell you—she's a whole lot and not
a little crazy—she's having therapy, has apparently very
seriously flipped only very recently, something to do

with Julien, has been having therapy but not showing up, sits or lies down reading or doing nothing but staring at the ceiling all day long in her place, eighteen dollars a month in Heavenly Lane, gets, apparently, some kind of allowance tied up somehow by her doctors or somebody with her inadequacy to work or something— is always talking about it and really too much for my likings—has apparently real hallucinations concerning nuns in the orphanage where she was raised and has seen them and felt actual threat—and also other things, like the sensation of taking junk although she's never had junk but only known junkies." —"Julien?"—"Julien takes junk whenever he can which is not often because he has no money and his ambition like is to be a real junky—but in any case she had hallucinations of not being properly contact high but actually somehow secretly injected by someone or something, people who follow her down the street, say, and is really crazy—and it's too much for me—and finally being a Negro I don't want to get all involved."—"Is she pretty?"—"Beautiful— but I can't make it."—"But boy I sure dig her looks and everything else."—"Well allright man then you'll make it— go over there, I'll give you the address, or better yet when, I'll invite her here and we'll talk, you can try if you want but although I have a hot feeling sexually and all that for her I really don't want to get any further into her not only for these reasons but finally, the big one, if I'm going to get involved with a girl now I want to be permanent like permanent and serious and long termed and I can't do that with her."—"I'd like a long permanent, et cetera."—"Well we'll see."

He told me of a night she'd be coming for a little snack dinner he'd cook for her so I was there, smoking tea in the red livingroom, with a dim red bulb light on, and she came in looking the same but now I was wearing a plain blue silk sports shirt and fancy slacks and I sat back cool to pretend to be cool hoping she would notice this with the result, when the lady entered the parlor I did not rise.

While they ate in the kitchen I pretended to read. I pretended to pay no attention whatever. We went out for a walk the three of us and by now all of us vying to talk like three good friends who want to get in and say everything on their minds, a friendly rivalry—we went to the Red Drum to hear the jazz which that night was Charlie Parker with Honduras Jones on drums and others interesting, probably Roger Beloit too, whom I wanted to see now, and that excitement of softnight San Francisco bop in the air but all in the cool sweet unexerting Beach—so we in fact ran, from Adam's on Telegraph Hill, down the white street under lamps, ran, jumped, showed off, had fun—felt gleeful and something was throbbing and I was pleased that she was able to walk as fast as we were—a nice thin strong little beauty to cut along the street with and so striking everyone turned to see, the strange bearded Adam, dark Mardou in strange slacks, and me, big gleeful hood.

So there we were at the Red Drum, a tableful of beers a few that is and all the gangs cutting in and out, paying a dollar quarter at the door, the little hip-pretending weasel there taking tickets, Paddy Cordavan floating in as prophesied (a big tall blond brakeman type subterranean from Eastern Washington cowboy-looking in jeans coming in to a wild generation party all smoky and mad and I yelled "Paddy Cordavan?" and "Yeah?" and he'd come over)—all sitting together, interesting groups at various tables, Julien, Roxanne (a woman of 25 prophesying the future style of America with short almost crewcut but with curls black snaky hair, snaky walk, pale pale junky anemic face and we say junky when once Dostoevski would have said what? if not ascetic or saintly? but not in the least? but the cold pale booster face of the cold blue girl and wearing a man's white shirt but with the cuffs undone untied at the buttons so I remember her leaning over talking to someone after having slinked across the floor with flowing propelled shoulders, bending to talk with her hand holding a short butt and the neat little flick she was giving it to knock ashes but repeatedly with long long fingernails an inch long and also orient and snake-like)—groups of all kinds, and Ross Wallenstein, the crowd, and up on the stand Bird Parker with solemn eyes who'd been busted fairly recently and had now returned to a kind of bop dead Frisco but had just discovered or been told about the Red Drum, the great new generation gang wailing and gathering there, so here he was on the stand, examining them with his eyes as he blew his now-settled-down-into-regulated-design "crazy" notes—the booming drums, the high ceiling—Adam for my sake dutifully cutting out at about 11 o'clock so he could go to bed and get to work in the morning, after a brief cutout with Paddy and myself for a quick ten-cent beer at roaring Pantera's, where Paddy and I in our first talk and laughter together pulled wrists—now Mardou cut out with me, glee eyed, between sets, for quick beers, but at her insistence at the Mask instead where they were fifteen cents, but she had a few pennies herself and we went there and began earnestly talking and getting hightingled on the beer and now it was the beginning—returning to the Red Drum for sets, to hear Bird, whom I saw distinctly digging Mardou several times also myself directly into my eye looking to search if really I was that great writer I thought myself to be as if he knew my thoughts and ambitions or remembered me from other night clubs and other coasts, other Chicagos—not a challenging look but the king and founder of the bop generation at least the sound of it in digging his audience digging his eyes, the secret eyes him-watching, as he just pursed his lips and let great lungs and immortal fingers work, his eyes separate and interested and humane, the kindest jazz musician there could be while being and therefore naturally the greatest—watching Mardou and me in the infancy of our love and probably wondering why, or knowing it wouldn't last, or seeing who it was would be hurt, as now, obviously, but not quite yet, it was Mardou whose eyes were shining in my direction, though I could not have known and now do not definitely know—except the one fact, on the way home, the session over the beer in the Mask drunk we went home on the Third Street bus sadly through night and throb knock neons and when I suddenly leaned over her to shout something further (in her secret self as later confessed) her heart leapt to smell the "sweetness of my breath" (quote) and suddenly she almost loved me—I not knowing this, as we found the Russian dark sad door of Heavenly Lane a great iron gate rasping on the sidewalk to the pull, the insides of smelling garbage cans sad-leaning together, fish heads, cats, and then the Lane itself, my first view of it (the long history and hugeness of it in my soul, as in 1951 cutting along with my sketchbook on a wild October evening when I was discovering my own writing soul at last I saw the subterranean Victor who'd come to Big Sur once on a motorcycle, was reputed to have gone to Alaska on same, with little subterranean chick Dorie Kiehl, there he was in striding Jesus coat heading north to Heavenly Lane to his pad and I followed him awhile, wondering about Heavenly Lane and all the long talks I'd been having for years with people like Mac Jones about the mystery, the silence of the subterraneans, "urban Thoreaus" Mac called them, as from Alfred Kazin in New York New School lectures back East commenting on all the students being interested in Whitman from a sexual revolution standpoint and in Thoreau from a contemplative mystic and antimaterialistic as if existentialist or whatever standpoint, the *Pierre*-of-Melville goof and wonder of it, the dark little beat burlap dresses, the stories you'd heard about great tenormen shooting junk by broken windows and starting at their horns, or great young poets with beats lying high in Rouault-like saintly obscurities, Heavenly Lane the famous Heavenly Lane where they'd all at one time or another the beat subterraneans lived, like Alfred and his little sickly wife something straight out of Dostoevski's Petersburg slums you'd think but really the American lost bearded idealistic—the whole thing in any case), seeing it for the first time, but with Mardou, the wash hung over the court, actually the back courtyard of a big 20-family tenement with bay windows, the wash hung out and in the afternoon the great symphony of Italian mothers, children, fathers BeFinneganing and yelling from stepladders, smells, cats mewing, Mexicans, the music from all the radios whether bolero of Mexican or Italian tenor of spaghetti eaters or loud suddenly turned-up KPFA symphonies of Vivaldi harpsichord intellectuals performances boom blam the tremendous sound of it which I then came to hear all the summer wrapt in the arms of my love—walking in there now, and going up the narrow musty stairs like in a hovel, and her door.

Plotting I demanded we dance—previously she'd been hungry so I'd suggested and we'd actually gone and bought egg foo young at Jackson and Kearny and now she heated this (later confession she'd hated it though it's one of my favorite dishes and typical of my later behavior I was already forcing down her throat that which she in subterranean sorrow wanted to endure alone if at all ever), ah.—Dancing, I had put the light out, so, in the dark, dancing, I kissed her—it was giddy, whirling to the dance, the beginning, the usual beginning of lovers kissing standing up in a dark room the room being the woman's the man all designs—ending up later in wild dances she on my lap or thigh as I danced her around bent back for balance and she around my neck her arms that came to warm so much the *me* that then was only hot—

And soon enough I'd learn she had no belief and had had no place to get it from—Negro mother dead for birth of her—unknown Cherokee-halfbreed father a hobo who'd come throwing torn shoes across gray plains of fall in black sombrero and pink scarf squatting by hotdog fires casting Tokay empties into the night "Yaa Calexico!"

Quick to plunge, bite, put the light out, hide my face in shame, make love to her tremendously because of lack of love for a year almost and the need pushing me down —our little agreements in the dark, the really should-not-be-tolds—for it was she who later said "Men are so crazy, they want the essence, the woman is the essence, there it is right in their hands but they rush off erecting big abstract constructions."—"You mean they should just stay home with the essence, that is lie under a tree all day with the woman but Mardou that's an old idea of mine, a lovely idea, I never heard it better expressed and never dreamed."—"Instead they rush off and have big wars and consider women as prizes instead of human beings, well man I may be in the middle of all this shit but I certainly don't want any part of it" (in her sweet cultured hip tones of new generation).—And so having had the essence of her love now I erect big word constructions and thereby betray it really—telling tales of every gossip sheet the washline of the world—and hers, ours, in all the two months of our love (I thought) only once-washed as she being a lonely subterranean spent mooningdays and would go to the laundry with them but suddenly it's dank late afternoon and too late and the sheets are gray, lovely to me—because soft.—But I cannot in this confession betray the innermosts, the thighs, what the thighs contain—and yet why write?—the thighs contain the essence—yet tho there I should stay and from there I came and'll eventually return, still I have to rush off and construct construct—for nothing—for Baudelaire poems—

Never did she use the word love, even that first moment after our wild dance when I carried her still on my lap and hanging clear to the bed and slowly dumped her, suffered to find her, which she loved, and being unsexual in her entire life (except for the first 15-year-old conjugality which for some reason consummated her and never since) (O the pain of telling these secrets which are so necessary to tell, or why write or live) now *"casus in eventu est"* but glad to have me losing my mind in the slight way egomaniacally I might on a few beers.— Lying then in the dark, soft, tentacled, waiting, till sleep —so in the morning I wake from the scream of beermares and see beside me the Negro woman with parted lips sleeping, and little bits of white pillow stuffing in her black hair, feel almost revulsion, realize what a beast I am for feeling anything near it, grape little sweetbody naked on the restless sheets of the nightbefore excitement, the noise in Heavenly Lane sneaking in through the gray windows, a gray doomsday in August so I feel like leaving at once to get "back to my work" the chimera of not the chimera but the orderly advancing sense of work and duty which I had worked up and developed at home (in South City) humble as it is, the comforts there too, the solitude which I wanted and now can't stand.—I got up and began to dress, apologize, she lay like a little mummy in the sheet and cast the serious brown eyes on me, like eyes of Indian watchfulness in a wood, like the brown lashes suddenly rising with black lashes to reveal sudden fantastic whites of eye with the brown glittering iris center, the seriousness of her face accentuated by the slightly Mongoloid as if of a boxer nose and the cheeks puffed a little from sleep, like the face on a beautiful porphyry mask found long ago and Aztecan.—"But why do you have to rush off so fast, as though almost hysterical or worried?"—"Well I do I have work to do and I have to straighten out—hangover—" and she barely awake, so I sneak out with a few words in fact when she lapses almost into sleep and I don't see her again for a few days—

The adolescent cocksman having made his conquest barely broods at home the loss of the love of the conquered lass, the blacklash lovely—no confession there.— It was on a morning when I slept at Adam's that I saw her again, I was going to rise, do some typing and coffee drinking in the kitchen all day since at that time work, work was my dominant thought, not love—not the pain which impels me to write this even while I don't want to, the pain which won't be eased by the writing of this but heightened, but which will be redeemed, and if only it were a dignified pain and could be placed somewhere other than in this black gutter of shame and loss and noisemaking folly in the night and poor sweat on my brow—Adam rising to go to work, I too, washing, mumbling talk, when the phone rang and it was Mardou, who was going to her therapist, but needed a dime for the bus, living around the corner, "Okay come on over but quick I'm going to work or I'll leave the dime with Leo."—"O is he there?"—"Yes."—In my mind man-thoughts of doing it again and actually looking forward to seeing her suddenly, as if I'd felt she was displeased with our first night (no reason to feel that, previous to the balling she'd lain on my chest eating the egg foo young and dug me with glittering glee eyes) (that tonight my enemy devour?) the thought of which makes me drop my greasy hot brow into a tired hand—O love, fled me—or do telepathies cross sympathetically in the night?—Such cacoëthes him befalls—that the cold lover of lust will earn the warm bleed of spirit—so she came in, 8 A.M., Adam went to work and we were alone and immediately she curled up in my lap, at my invite, in the big stuffed chair and we began to talk, she began to tell her story and I turned on (in the gray day) the dim red bulblight and thus began our true love—

She had to tell me everything—no doubt just the other day she'd already told her whole story to Adam and he'd listened tweaking his beard with a dream in his far-off eye to look attentive and loverman in the bleak eternity, nodding—now with me she was starting all over again but as if (as I thought) to a brother of Adam's a greater lover and bigger, more awful listener and worrier.—There we were in all gray San Francisco of the gray West, you could almost smell rain in the air and far across the land, over the mountains beyond Oakland and out beyond Donner and Truckee was the great desert of Nevada, the wastes leading to Utah, to Colorado, to the cold cold come fall plains where I kept

imagining that Cherokee-halfbreed hobo father of hers
lying bellydown on a flatcar with the wind furling back
his rags and black hat, his brown sad face facing all that
land and desolation.—At other moments I imagined him
instead working as a picker around Indio and on a hot
night he's sitting on a chair on the sidewalk among the
joking shirtsleeved men, and he spits and they say, "Hey
Hawk Taw, tell us that story agin about the time you
stole a taxicab and drove it clear to Manitoba, Canada—
d'jever hear him tell that one, Cy?"—I saw the vision
of her father, he's standing straight up, proudly, hand-
some, in the bleak dim red light of America on a corner,
nobody knows his name, nobody cares—

Her own little stories about flipping and her minor
fugues, cutting across boundaries of the city, and
smoking too much marijuana, which held so much terror
for her (in the light of my own absorptions concerning
her father the founder of her flesh and predecessor ter-
ror-ee of her terrors and knower of much greater flips
and madness than she in psychoanalytic-induced anxieties
could ever even summon up to just imagine), formed just
the background for thoughts about the Negroes and
Indians and America in general but with all the over-
tones of "new generation" and other historical concerns
in which she was now swirled just like all of us in the
Wig and Europe Sadness of us all, the innocent seriousness with which she told her story and I'd listened to
so often and myself told—wide-eyed hugging in heaven

together—hipsters of America in the 1950's sitting in a
dim room—the clash of the streets beyond the window's
bare soft sill.—Concern for her father, because I'd been
out there and sat down on the ground and seen the rail
the steel of America covering the ground filled with the
bones of old Indians and Original Americans.—In the
cold gray fall in Colorado and Wyoming I'd worked on
the land and watched Indian hoboes come suddenly out
of brush by the track and move slowly, hawk lipped, rill-
jawed and wrinkled, into the great shadow of the light
bearing burdenbags and junk talking quietly to one another and so distant from the absorptions of the field
hands, even the Negroes of Cheyenne and Denver streets,
the Japs, the general minority Armenians and Mexicans
of the whole West that to look at a three-or-foursome of
Indians crossing a field and a railroad track is to the
senses like something unbelievable as a dream—you
think, "They must be Indians—ain't a soul looking at
'em—they're goin' that way—nobody notices—doesn't matter much which way they go—reservation? What have
they got in those brown paper bags?" and only with a
great amount of effort you realize "But they were the
inhabitors of this land and under these huge skies they
were the worriers and keeners and protectors of wives
in whole nations gathered around tents—now the rail
that runs over their forefathers' bones leads them onward
pointing into infinity, wraiths of humanity treading lightly
the surface of the ground so deeply suppurated with the

stock of their suffering you only have to dig a foot down
to find a baby's hand.—The hotshot passenger train with
grashing diesel balls by, browm, browm, the Indians just
look up—I see them vanishing like spots—" and sitting in
the redbulb room in San Francisco now with sweet
Mardou I think, "And this is your father I saw in the gray
waste, swallowed by night—from his juices came your
lips, your eyes full of suffering and sorrow, and we're not
to know his name or name his destiny?"—Her little brown
hand is curled in mine, her fingernails are paler than her
skin, on her toes too and with her shoes off she has one
foot curled in between my thighs for warmth and we talk,
we begin our romance on the deeper level of love and
histories of respect and shame.—For the greatest key to
courage is shame and the blurfaces in the passing train
see nothing out on the plain but figures of hoboes rolling
out of sight—

"I remember one Sunday, Mike and Rita were over,
we had some very strong tea—they said it had volcanic
ash in it and it was the strongest they'd ever had."—
"Came from L. A.?"— "From Mexico—some guys had
driven down in the station wagon and pooled their
money, or Tijuana or something, I dunno—Rita was flipping at the time—when we were practically stoned she
rose very dramatically and stood there in the middle of
the room man saying she felt her nerves burning thru
her bones—To see her *flip* right before my eyes—I got
nervous and had some kind of idea about Mike, he kept

looking at me like he wanted to kill me—he has such a
funny look anyway—I got out of the house and walked
along and didn't know which way to go, my mind kept
turning into the several directions that I was thinking of
going but my body kept walking straight along Columbus altho I felt the sensation of each of the directions I
mentally and emotionally turned into, amazed at all the
possible directions you can take with different motives
that come in, like it can make you a different *person*—
I've often thought of this since childhood, of suppose
instead of going up Columbus as I usually did I'd turn
into Filbert would something happen that at the time is
insignificant enough but would be like enough to influence my whole life in the end?—What's in store for me
in the direction I *don't* take?—and all that, so if this had
not been such a constant preoccupation that accompanied
me in my solitude which I played upon in as many different ways as possible I wouldn't bother now except
but seeing the horrible roads this pure *supposing* goes
to it took me to *frights,* if I wasn't so damned *persistent*
—" and so on deep into the day, a long confusing story
only pieces of which and imperfectly I remember, just
the mass of the misery in connective form—

Flips in gloomy afternoons in Julien's room and Julien
sitting paying no attention to her but staring in the gray
moth void stirring only occasionally to close the window
or change his knee crossings, eyes round staring in a
meditation so long and so mysterious and as I say so

Christlike really outwardly lamby it was enough to drive
anybody crazy I'd say to live there even one day with
Julien or Wallenstein (same type) or Mike Murphy
(same type), the subterraneans their gloomy long-
thoughts enduring.—And the meekened girl waiting in a
dark corner, as I remembered so well the time I was at
Big Sur and Victor arrived on his literally homemade
motorcycle with little Dorie Kiehl, there was a party in
Patsy's cottage, beer, candlelight, radio, talk, yet for the
first hour the newcomers in their funny ragged clothes
and he with that beard and she with those somber
serious eyes had sat practically out of sight behind the
candlelight shadows so no one could see them and since
they said nothing whatever but just (if not listened)
meditated, gloomed, endured, finally I even forgot they
were there—and later that night they slept in a pup tent
in the field in the foggy dew of Pacific Coast Starry Night
and with the same humble silence mentioned nothing in
the morn—Victor so much in my mind always the central
exaggerator of subterranean hip generation tendencies to
silence, bohemian mystery, drugs, beard, semiholiness
and, as I came to find later, insurpassable nastiness (like
George Sanders in *The Moon and Sixpence*)—so Mardou
a healthy girl in her own right and from the windy
open ready for love now hid in a musty corner waiting
for Julien to speak.—Occasionally in the general "incest"
she'd been slyly silently by some consenting arrangement
or secret statesmanship shifted or probably just "Hey

Ross you take Mardou home tonight I wanta make it with Rita for a change,"—and staying at Ross's for a week, smoking the volcanic ash, she was flipping—(the tense anxiety of improper sex additionally, the premature ejaculations of these anemic *maquereaux* leaving her suspended in tension and wonder).—"I was just an innocent chick when I met them, independent and like well not happy or anything but feeling that I had something to do, I wanted to go to night school, I had several jobs at my trade, binding in Olstad's and small places down around Harrison, the art teacher the old gal at school was saying I could become a great sculptress and I was living with various roommates and buying clothes and making it" (sucking in her little lip, and that slick 'cuk' in the throat of drawing in breath quickly in sadness and as if with a cold, like in the throats of great drinkers, but she not a drinker but saddener of self) (supreme, dark)—(twining warm arm farther around me) "and he's lying there saying whatsamatter and I can't understand—." She can't understand suddenly what has happened because she's lost her mind, her usual recognition of self, and feels the eerie buzz of mystery, she really does not know who she is and what for and where she is, she looks out the window and this city San Francisco is the big bleak bare stage of some giant joke being perpetrated on her.—"With my back turned I didn't know what Ross was thinking—even doing."—She had no clothes on, she'd risen out of his satisfied sheets to stand in the wash of gray gloomtime thinking what to do, where to go.—And the longer she stood there finger-in-mouth and the more the man said, "What's the matter ba-by" (finally he stopped asking and just let her stand there) the more she could feel the pressure from inside towards bursting and explosion coming on, finally she took a giant step forward with a gulp of fear—everything was clear: danger in the air—it was writ in the shadows, in the gloomy dust behind the drawing table in the corner, in the garbage bags, the gray drain of day seeping down the wall and into the window—in the hollow eyes of people—she ran out of the room.—"What'd he say?"

"Nothing—he didn't move but was just with his head off the pillow when I glanced back in closing the door— I had no clothes on in the alley, it didn't disturb me, I was so intent on this realization of everything I knew I was an innocent child."—"The naked babe, wow."—(And to myself: "My God, this girl, Adam's right she's crazy, like I'd do that, I'd flip like I did on Benzedrine with Honey in 1945 and thought she wanted to use my body for the gang car and the wrecking and flames but I'd certainly never run out into the streets of San Francisco naked tho I might have maybe if I really felt there was need for action, yah") and I looked at her wondering if she, was she telling the truth.—She was in the alley, wondering who she was, night, a thin drizzle of mist, si-lence of sleeping Frisco, the B-O boats in the bay, the shroud over the bay of great clawmouth fogs, the aureola of funny eerie light being sent up in the middle by the Arcade Hood Droops of the Pillar-templed Alcatraz—her heart thumping in the stillness, the cool dark peace.—Up on a wood fence, waiting—to see if some idea from outside would be sent telling her what to do next and full of import and omen because it had to be right and just once—"One slip in the wrong direction . . . ," her direction kick, should she jump down on one side of fence or other, endless space reaching out in four directions, bleak-hatted men going to work in glistening streets uncaring of the naked girl hiding in the mist or if they'd been there and seen her would in a circle stand not touching her just waiting for the cop-authorities to come and cart her away and all their uninterested weary eyes flat with blank shame watching every part of her body—the naked babe. —The longer she hangs on the fence the less power she'll have finally to really get down and decide, and upstairs Ross Wallenstein doesn't even move from that junk-high bed, thinking her in the hall huddling, or he's gone to sleep anyhow in his own skin and bone.—The rainy night blooping all over, kissing everywhere men women and cities in one wash of sad poetry, with honey lines of high-shelved Angels trumpet-blowing up above the final Orient-shroud Pacific-huge songs of Paradise, an end to fear below.—She squats on the fence, the thin drizzle making beads on her brown shoulders, stars in her hair, her wild now-Indian eyes now staring into the Black with a little fog emanating from her brown mouth, the misery like ice crystals on the blankets on the ponies of her Indian ancestors, the drizzle on the village long ago and the poorsmoke crawling out of the underground and when a mournful mother pounded acorns and made mush in hopeless millenniums—the song of the Asia hunting gang clanking down the final Alaskan rib of earth to New World Howls (in their eyes and in Mardou's eyes now the eventual Kingdom of Inca Maya and vast Azteca shining of gold snake and temples as noble as Greek, Egypt, the long sleek crack jaws and flattened noses of Mongolian geniuses creating arts in temple rooms and the leap of their jaws to speak, till the Cortez Spaniards, the Pizarro weary old-world sissified pantalooned Dutch bums came smashing canebrake in savannahs to find shining cities of Indian Eyes high, landscaped, boulevarded, ritualled, heralded, beflagged in that selfsame New World Sun the beating heart held up to it)—her heart beating in the Frisco rain, on the fence, facing last facts, ready to go run down the land now and go back and fold in again where she was and where was all—consoling herself with visions of truth—coming down off the fence, on tiptoe moving ahead, finding a hall, shuddering, sneaking—

"I'd make up my mind, I'd erected some structure, it was like, but I can't—." Making a new start, starting from flesh in the rain, "Why should anyone want to harm my little heart, my feet, my little hands, my skin that I'm

wrapt in because God wants me warm and Inside, my
toes—why did God make all this all so decayable and
dieable and harmable and wants to make me realize and
scream—why the wild ground and bodies bare and breaks
—I quaked when the giver creamed, when my father
screamed, my mother dreamed—I started small and bal-
looned up and now I'm big and a naked child again and
only to cry and fear. —Ah—Protect yourself, angel of no
harm, you who've never and could never harm and crack
another innocent its shell and thin veiled pain—wrap
a robe around you, honey lamb—protect yourself from
rain and wait, till Daddy comes again, and Mama throws
you warm inside her valley of the moon, loom at the loom
of patient time, be happy in the mornings."—Making a
new start, shivering, out of the alley night naked in the
skin and on wood feet to the stained door of some
neighbor—knocking—the woman coming to the door in
answer to the frightened butter knock knuckles, sees the
naked browngirl, frightened—("Here is a woman, a soul
in my rain, she looks at me, she is frightened.")—"Knocking on this perfect stranger's door, sure."—"Thinking I
was just going down the street to Betty's and back,
promised her *meaning* it deeply I'd bring the clothes
back and she did let me in and she got a blanket and
wrapped it around me, then the clothes, and luckily she
was alone—an Italian woman.—And in the alley I'd all
come out and *on*, it was now first clothes, then I'd go to
Betty's and get two bucks—then buy this brooch I'd seen

that afternoon at some place with old seawood in the window, at North Beach, art handicraft ironwork like, a shoppey, it was the first symbol I was going to allow myself."—"Sure."—Out of the naked rain to a robe, to innocence shrouding in, then the decoration of God and religious sweetness.—"Like when I had that fist fight with Jack Steen it was in my mind strongly."—"Fist fight with Jack Steen?"—"This was earlier, all the junkies in Ross's room, tying up and shooting with Pusher, you know Pusher, well I took my clothes off there too—it was . . . all . . . part of the same . . . flip . . ."—"But this *clothes,* this *clothes!*" (to myself).—"I stood in the middle of the room flipping and Pusher was plucking at the guitar, just one string, and I went up to him and said, 'Man don't pluck those dirty notes at ME,' and like he just got up without a word and left."—And Jack Steen was furious at her and thought if he hit her and knocked her out with his fists she'd come to her senses so he slugged at her but she was just as strong as he (anemic pale 110 lb. junky ascetics of America), blam, they fought it out before the weary others.—She'd pulled wrists with Jack, Julien, beat them practically—"Like Julien finally won at wrists but he really furiously had to put me down to do it and hurt me and was really upset" (gleeful little shniffle thru the little out-teeth)—so there she'd been fighting it out with Jack Steen and really almost licking him but he was furious and neighbors downstairs called cops who came and had to be explained to

—"dancing."—"But that day I'd seen this iron thing, a little brooch with a beautiful dull sheen, to be worn around the neck, you know how nice that would look on my breast."—"On your brown breastbone a dull gold beautiful it would be baby, go on with your amazing story."—"So I immediately needed this brooch in spite of the time, 4 A.M. now, and I had that old coat and shoes and an old dress she gave me, I felt like a streetwalker but I felt no one could tell—I ran to Betty's for the two bucks, woke her up—." She demanded the money, she was coming out of death and money was just the means to get the shiny brooch (the silly means invented by inventors of barter and haggle and styles of who owns who, who owns what—). Then she was running down the street with her $2, going to the store long before it opened, going for coffee in the cafeteria, sitting at the table alone, digging the world at last, the gloomy hats, the glistening sidewalks, the signs announcing baked flounder, the reflections of rain in paneglass and in pillar mirror, the beauty of the food counters displaying cold spreads and mountains of crullers and the steam of the coffee urn.— "How warm the world is, all you gotta do is get little symbolic coins—they'll let you in for all the warmth and food you want—you don't have to strip your skin off and chew your bone in alleyways—these places were designed to house and comfort bag-and-bone people come to cry for consolation."—She is sitting there staring at everyone, the usual sexfiends are afraid to stare back because the vibration from her eyes is wild, they sense some living danger in the apocalypse of her tense avid neck and trembling wiry hands.—"This ain't no woman."—"That crazy Indian she'll kill somebody."—Morning coming, Mardou hurrying gleeful and mindswum, absorbed, to the store, to buy the brooch—standing then in a drugstore at the picture postcard swiveller for a solid two hours examining each one over and over again minutely because she only had ten cents left and could only buy two and those two must be perfect private talismans of the new important meaning, personal omen emblems—her avid lips slack to see the little corner meanings of the cable-car shadows, Chinatown, flower stalls, blue, the clerks wondering: "Two hours she's been in here, no stockings on, dirty knees, looking at cards, some Third Street Wino's wife run away, came to the big whiteman drug-store, never saw a shiny sheen postcard before—." In the night before they would have seen her up Market Street in Foster's with her last (again) dime and a glass of milk, crying into her milk, and men always looking at her, always trying to make her but now doing nothing because frightened, because she was like a child—and because: "Why didn't Julien or Jack Steen or Walt Fitzpatrick give you a place to stay and leave you alone in the corner, or lend you a couple bucks?"—"But they didn't care, they were frightened of me, they *really* didn't want me around, they had like distant objectivity, watching me, asking *nasty* questions—a couple times Julien went into his head-against-mine act like you know 'Whatsamatter, Mardou,' and his routines like that and phony sympathy but he really just was curious to find out why I was flipping—none of them'd ever give me *money*, man."—"Those guys really treated you bad, do you know that?" —"Yeah well they never treat anyone—like they never do anything—you take care of yourself, I'll take care of me."—"Existentialism."—"But American worse cool existentialism and of junkies man, I hung around with them, it was for almost a year by then and I was getting, every time they turned on, a kind of a contact high."— She'd sit with them, they'd go on the nod, in the dead silence she'd wait, sensing the slow snakelike waves of vibration struggling across the room, the eyelids falling, the heads nodding and jerking up again, someone mumbling some disagreeable complaint, "Ma-a-n, I'm drug by that son of a bitch MacDoud with all his routines about how he ain't got enough money for one cap, could he get a half a cap or pay a half—m-a-a-n, I never seen such nowhereness, no s-h-i-t, why don't he just go somewhere and *fade*, um." (That junkey 'um' that follows any out-on-the-limb, and anything one says is out-on-the-limb, statement, *um, he-um*, the self-indulgent baby sob inkept from exploding to the big bawl mawk crackfaced WAAA they feel from the junk regressing their systems to the crib.)—Mardou would be sitting there, and finally high on tea or benny she'd begin to feel like she'd been injected, she'd walk down the street in her flip and actually

[40]

feel the electric contact with other human beings (in her sensitivity recognizing a fact) but some times she was suspicious because it was someone secretly injecting her and following her down the street who was really responsible for the electric sensation and so independent of any natural law of the universe.—"But you really didn't believe that—but you did—when I flipped on benny in 1945 I really believed the girl wanted to use my body to burn it and put her boy's papers in my pocket so the cops'd think he was dead—I told her, too."—"Oh what did she do?"—"She said, 'Ooo daddy,' and hugged me and took care of me, Honey was a wild bitch, she put pancake makeup on my pale—I'd lost thirty, ten, fifteen pounds—but what happened?"—"I wandered around with my brooch."—She went into some kind of gift shop and there was a man in a wheel chair there. (She wandered into a doorway with cages and green canaries in the glass, she wanted to touch the beads, watch goldfish, caress the old fat cat sunning on the floor, stand in the cool green parakeet jungle of the store high on the green out-of-this-world dart eyes of parrots swiveling witless necks to cake and burrow in the mad feather and to feel that definite communication from them of birdy terror, the electric spasms of their notice, s q u a w k, l a w k, l e e k, and the man was extremely strange.)—"Why?"—"I dunno he was just very strange, he wanted, he talked with me very clearly and insisting—like intensely looking right at me and at great length but smiling about the simplest

[41]

commonplace subjects but we both knew we meant everything else that we said—you know life—actually it was
about the tunnels, the Stockton Street tunnel and the one
they just built on Broadway, that's the one we talked of
the most, but as we talked this a great electrical current
of real understanding passed between us and I could feel
the other levels the infinite number of them of every
intonation in his speech and mine and the world of
meaning in every *word*—I'd never realized before how
much is *happening* all the time, and people *know* it—in
their eyes they show it, they *refuse* to show it by any
other—I stayed a very long time."—"He must have been
a weirdy himself."—"You know, balding, and queer like,
and middleaged, and with that with-neck-cut-off look
or head-on-air," (witless, peaked) "looking all over, I
guess it was his mother the old lady with the Paisley shawl
—but my god it would take me all day."—"Wow."—"Out
on the street this beautiful old woman with white hair
had come up to me and saw me, but was asking directions, but liked to talk—." (On the sunny now lyrical
Sunday morning after-rain sidewalk, Easter in Frisco and
all the purple hats out and the lavender coats parading
in the cool gusts and the little girls so tiny with their
just whitened shoes and hopeful coats going slowly in the
white hill streets, churches of old bells busy and down-
town around Market where our tattered holy Negro Joan
of Arc wandered hosannahing in her brown borrowed-
from-night skin and heart, flutters of betting sheets at

corner newsstands, watchers at nude magazines, the flowers on the corner in baskets and the old Italian in his apron with the newspapers kneeling to water, and the Chinese father in tight ecstatic suit wheeling the basket-carriaged baby down Powell with his pink-spot-cheeked wife of glitter brown eyes in her new bonnet rippling to flap in sun, there stands Mardou smiling intensely and strangely and the old eccentric lady not any more conscious of her Negroness than the kind cripple of the store and because of her out and open face now, the clear indications of a troubled pure innocent spirit just risen from a pit in pockmarked earth and by own broken hands self-pulled to safety and salvation, the two women Mardou and the old lady in the incredibly sad empty streets of Sunday after the excitements of Saturday night the great glitter up and down Market like wash gold dusting and the throb of neons at O'Farrell and Mason bars with cocktail glass cherrysticks winking invitation to the open hungering hearts of Saturday and actually leading only finally to Sunday-morning blue emptiness just the flutter of a few papers in the gutter and the long white view to Oakland Sabbath haunted, still—Easter sidewalk of Frisco as white ships cut in clean blue lines from Sasebo beneath the Golden Gate's span, the wind that sparkles all the leaves of Marin here laving the washed glitter of the white kind city, in the lostpurity clouds high above redbrick track and Embarcadero pier, the haunted broken hint of song of old Pomos the once

only-wanderers of these eleven last American now white-
behoused hills, the face of Mardou's father himself now
as she raises her face to draw breath to speak in the
streets of life materializing huge above America, fad-
ing—.) "And like I told her but talked too and when
she left she gave me her flower and pinned it on me
and called me honey."—"Was she white?"—"Yeah, like, she
was very affectionate, very plea-*sant* she seemed to love
me—like save me, bring me out—I walked up a hill, up
California past Chinatown, someplace I came to a white
garage like with a big garage wall and this guy in a
swivel chair wanted to know what I wanted, I under-
stood all of my moves as one obligation after another to
communicate to whoever not accidentally but by *arrangement* was placed before me, communicate and exchange
this news, the vibration and new meaning that I had,
about everything happening to everyone all the time
everywhere and for them not to worry, nobody as mean
as you think or—a colored guy, in the swivel chair, and
we had a long confused talk and he was reluctant, I
remember, to look in my eyes and really listen to what I
was saying."—"But what were you saying?"—"But it's all
forgotten now—something as simple and like you'd never
expect like those tunnels or the old lady and I hanging-up
on streets and directions—but the guy wanted to make it
with me, I saw him open his zipper but suddenly he got
ashamed, I was turned around and could see it in the
glass." (In the white planes of wall garage morning, the

phantom man and the girl turned slumped watching in
the window that not only reflected the black strange
sheepish man secretly staring but the whole office, the
chair, the safe, the dank concrete back interiors of garage and dull sheen autos, showing up also unwashed
specks of dust from last night's rainsplash and thru
the glass the across-the-street immortal balcony of
wooden bay-window tenement where suddenly she saw
three Negro children in strange attire waving but without
yelling at a Negro man four stories below in overalls and
therefore apparently working on Easter, who waved back
as he walked in his own strange direction that bisected
suddenly the slow direction being taken by two men, two
hatted, coated ordinary men but carrying one a bottle,
the other a boy of three, stopping now and then to raise
the bottle of Four Star California Sherry and drink as
the Frisco A.M. All Morn Sun wind flapped their tragic
topcoats to the side, the boy bawling, their shadows
on the street like shadows of gulls the color of handmade
Italian cigars of deep brown stores at Columbus and
Pacific, now the passage of a fishtail Cadillac in second
gear headed for hilltop houses bay-viewing and some
scented visit of relatives bringing the funny papers, news
of old aunts, candy to some unhappy little boy waiting
for Sunday to end, for the sun to cease pouring thru the
French blinds and paling the potted plants but rather
rain and Monday again and the joy of the woodfence
alley where only last night poor Mardou'd almost lost.)

The Subterraneans

—"What'd the colored guy do?"—"He zipped up again, he wouldn't look at me, he turned away, it was strange he got ashamed and sat down—it reminded me too when I was a little girl in Oakland and this man would send us to the store and give us dimes then he'd open his bathrobe and show us himself."—"Negro?"—"Yea, in my neighborhood where I lived—I remember I used to never stay there but my girfriend did and I think she even did something with him one time."—"What'd you do about the guy in the swivel chair?"—"Well, like I wandered out of there and it was a beautiful day, Easter, man."— "Gad, Easter where was I?"—"The soft sun, the flowers and here I was going down the street and thinking 'Why did I allow myself to be bored ever in the past and to compensate for it got high or drunk or rages or all the tricks people have because they want anything but serene understanding of just what there is, which is after all so much, and thinking like angry social deals,—like angry— kicks—like hassling over social problems and my race problem, it meant so little and I could feel that great confidence and gold of the morning would slip away eventually and had already started—I could have made my whole life like that morning just on the strength of pure understanding and willingness to live and go along, God it was all the most beautiful thing that ever happened to me in its own way—but it was all sinister."— Ended when she got home to her sisters' house in Oakland and they were furious at her anyway but she told

them off and did strange things; she noticed for instance
the complicated wiring her eldest sister had done to
connect the TV and the radio to the kitchen plug in the
ramshackle wood upstairs of their cottage near Seventh
and Pine the railroad sooty wood and gargoyle porches
like tinder in the sham scrapple slums, the yard nothing
but a lot with broken rocks and black wood showing
where hoboes Tokay'd last night before moving off
across the meatpacking yard to the Mainline rail Tracy-
bound thru vast endless impossible Brooklyn-Oakland
full of telephone poles and crap and on Saturday nights
the wild Negro bars full of whores and the Mexicans
Ya-Yaaing in their own saloons and the cop car cruising
the long sad avenue riddled with drinkers and the glitter
of broken bottles (now in the wood house where she was
raised in terror Mardou is squatting against the wall
looking at the wires in the half dark and she hears herself
speak and doesn't understand why she's saying it except
that it must be said, come out, because that day earlier
when in her wandering she finally got to wild Third
Street among the lines of slugging winos and the bloody
drunken Indians with bandages rolling out of alleys and
the 10¢ movie house with three features and little children of skid row hotels running on the sidewalk and the
pawnshops and the Negro chickenshack jukeboxes and
she stood in drowsy sun suddenly listening to bop as if
for the first time as it poured out, the intention of the
musicians and of the horns and instruments suddenly

a mystical unity expressing itself in waves like sinister
and again electricity but screaming with palpable alive-
ness the direct *word* from the vibration, the interchanges
of statement, the levels of waving intimation, the smile
in sound, the same living insinuation in the way her
sister'd arranged those wires wriggled entangled and
fraught with intention, innocent looking but actually behind the mask of casual life completely by agreement
the mawkish mouth almost sneering snakes of electricity
purposely placed she'd been seeing all day and hearing
in the music and saw now in the wires), "What are you
trying to do actually electrocute me?" so the sisters could
see something was really wrong, worse than the youngest
of the Fox sisters who was alcoholic and made the wild
street and got arrested regularly by the vice squad, some
nameless horrible yawning *wrong*, "She smokes dope,
she hangs out with all those queer guys with beards in
the City."—They called the police and Mardou was taken
to the hospital—realizing now, "God, I saw how awful
what was really happening and about to happen to me
and man I pulled out of it fast, and talked sanely with
everyone possible and did everything right, they let me
out in 48 hours—the other women were with me, we'd
look out the windows and the things they said, they made
me see the preciousness of really being *out* of those damn
bathrobes and *out* of there and out on the street, the sun,
we could see ships, out and FREE man to roam around,
how great it really is and how we never appreciate it all

glum inside our worries and skins, like *fools* really, or
blind spoiled destestable children pouting because . . .
they can't get . . . all . . . the . . . candy . . . they want,
so I talked to the doctors and told them—." "And you had
no place to stay, where was your clothes?"—"Scattered
all over—all over the Beach—I had to do something—they
let me have this place, some friends of mine, for the
summer, I'll have to get out in October."—"In the Lane?"
—"Yah."—"Honey let's you and me—would you go to
Mexico with me?"—"Yes!"—"If I go to Mexico? that is, if
I get the money? altho I do have a hunnerd eighty now
and we really actually could go tomorrow and make it
—like Indians—I mean cheap and living in the country
or in the slums."—"Yes—it would be so nice to get away
now."—"But we could or should really wait till I get—
I'm supposed to get five hundred see—and—" (and that
was when I would have whisked her off into the bosom
of my own life)—she saying "I really don't want anything
more to do with the Beach or any of that gang, man,
that's why—I guess I spoke or agreed too soon, you don't
seem so sure now" (laughing to see me ponder).—"But
I'm only pondering practical problems."—"Nevertheless
if I'd have said 'maybe' I bet—oooo that awright," kissing
me—the gray day, the red bulblight, I had never heard
such a story from such a soul except from the great men
I had known in my youth, great heroes of America I'd
been buddies with, with whom I'd adventured and gone
to jail and known in raggedy dawns, the boys beat on

curbstones seeing symbols in the saturated gutter, the
Rimbauds and Verlaines of America on Times Square,
kids—no girl had ever moved me with a story of spiritual
suffering and so beautifully her soul showing out radiant
as an angel wandering in hell and the hell the selfsame
streets I'd roamed in watching, watching for someone
just like her and never dreaming the darkness and the
mystery and eventuality of our meeting in eternity, the
hugeness of her face now like the sudden vast Tiger head
on a poster on the back of a woodfence in the smoky
dumpyards Saturday no-school mornings, direct, beautiful, insane, in the rain.—We hugged, we held close—it
was like love now, I was amazed—we made it in the
livingroom, gladly, in chairs, on the bed, slept entwined,
satisfied—I would show her more sexuality—

We woke up late, she'd not gone to her psychoanalyst,
she'd "wasted" her day and when Adam came home and
saw us in the chair again still talking and with the house
belittered (coffee cups, crumbs of cakes I'd bought down
on tragic Broadway in the gray Italianness which was so
much like the lost Indianness of Mardou, tragic America-
Frisco with its gray fences, gloomy sidewalks, doorways
of dank, I from the small town and more recently from
sunny Florida East Coast found so frightening).—"Mardou, you wasted your visit to a therapist, really Leo you
should be ashamed and feel a little responsible, after
all—" "You mean I'm making her lay off her duties . . .

I used to do it with all my girls . . . ah it'll be good for
her to miss" (not knowing her need).—Adam almost joking but also most serious, "Mardou you must write a
letter or call—why don't you call him now?"—"It's a she
doctor, up at City & County."—"Well call now, here's a
dime."—"But I can do it tomorrow, but it's too late."—
"How do you know it's too late—no really, you really
goofed today, and you too Leo you're awfully responsible
you rat." And then a gay supper, two girls coming from
outside (gray crazy outside) to join us, one of them fresh
from an overland drive from New York with Buddy Pond,
the doll an L.A. hip type with short haircut who immediately pitched into the dirty kitchen and cooked everybody a delicious supper of black bean soup (all out of
cans) with a few groceries while the other girl, Adam's,
goofed on the phone and Mardou and I sat around
guiltily, darkly in the kitchen drinking stale beer and
wondering if Adam wasn't perhaps really right about
what should be done, how one should pull oneself
together, but our stories told, our love solidified, and
something sad come into both our eyes—the evening pro-
ceeding with the gay supper, five of us, the girl with the
short haircut saying later that I was so beautiful she
couldn't look (which later turned out to be an East Coast
saying of hers and Buddy Pond's), "beautiful" so amazing to me, unbelievable, but must have impressed Mardou, who was anyway during the supper jealous of the
girl's attentions to me and later said so—my position so

airy, secure—and we all went driving in her foreign con-
vertible car, through now clearing Frisco streets not gray
but opening soft hot reds in the sky between the homes
Mardou and I lying back in the open backseat digging
them, the soft shades, commenting, holding hands—they
up front like gay young international Paris sets driving
through town, the short hair girl driving solemnly, Adam
pointing out—going to visit some guy on Russian Hill
packing for a New York train and France-bound ship
where a few beers, small talk, later troopings on foot with
Buddy Pond to some literary friend of Adam's Aylward
So-and-So famous for the dialogs in *Current Review*,
possessor of a magnificent library, then around the corner
to (as I told Aylward) America's greatest wit, Charles
Bernard, who had gin, and an old gray queer, and others,
and sundry suchlike parties, ending late at night as I
made my first foolish mistake in my life and love with
Mardou, refusing to go home with all the others at 3 A.M.,
insisting, tho at Charles' invite, to stay till dawn studying
his pornographic (homo male sexual) pictures and listening to Marlene Dietrich records, with Aylward—the
others leaving, Mardou tired and too much to drink looking at me meekly and not protesting and seeing how I
was, a drunk really, always staying late, freeloading,
shouting, foolish—but now loving me so not complaining
and on her little bare thonged brown feet padding around
the kitchen after me as we mix drinks and even when
Bernard claims a pornographic picture has been stolen

by her (as she's in the bathroom and he's telling me confidentially, "My dear, I saw her slip it into her pocket, her waist I mean her breast pocket") so that when she comes out of bathroom she senses some of this, the queers around her, the strange drunkard she's with, she complains not—the first of so many indignities piled on her, not on her capacity for suffering but gratuitously on her little female dignities.—Ah I shouldn't have done it, goofed, the long list of parties and drinkings and down-crashings and times I ran out on her, the final shocker being when in a cab together she's insisting I take her home (to sleep) and I can go see Sam alone (in bar) but I jump out of cab, madly ("I never saw anything so maniacal"), and run into another cab and zoom off, leaving her in the night—so when Yuri bangs on her door the following night, and I'm not around, and he's drunk and insists, and jumps on her as he'd been doing, she gave in, she gave in—she gave up—jumping ahead of my story, naming my enemy at once—the pain, why should "the sweet ram of their lunge in love" which has really nothing to do with me in time or space, be like a dagger in my throat?

Walking up, then, from the partying, in Heavenly Lane, again I have the beer nightmare (now a little gin too) and with remorse and again almost and now for no reason revulsion the little white woolly particles from the pillow stuffing in her black almost wiry hair, and her puffed cheeks and little puffed lips, the gloom and dank of Heavenly Lane, and once more "I gotta go home, straighten out"—as tho never I was straight with her, but crooked—never away from my chimerical workroom and comfort home, in the alien gray of the world city, in a state of WELL-BEING—. "But why do you always want to rush off so soon?"—"I guess a feeling of well-being at home, that I need, to be straight—like—." "I know baby—but I'm, I miss you in a way I'm jealous that you have a home and a mother who irons your clothes and all that and I haven't—." "When shall I come back, Friday night?" —"But baby it's up to you—to say when."—"But tell me what YOU want."—"But I'm not supposed to."—"But what do you mean s'posed?"—"It's like what they say—about—oh, I dunno" (sighing, turning over in the bed, hiding, burrowing little grape body around, so I go, turn her over, flop on bed, kiss the straight line that runs from her breastbone, a depression there, straight, clear down to her bellybutton where it becomes an infinitesimal line and proceeds like as if ruled with pencil on down and then continues just as straight underneath, and need a man get well-being from history and thought as she herself said when he has that, the essence, but still).—The weight of my need to go home, my neurotic fears, hangovers, horrors—"I shouldna—we shouldn't a gone to Bernard's at all last night—at least we shoulda come home at three with the others."—"That's what I say baby—but God" (laughing the shnuffle and making little funny imitation voice of slurring) "you never do what I ash you

t'do."—"Aw I'm sorry—I love you—do you love me?"—
"Man," laughing, "what do you *mean*"—looking at me
warily—"I mean do you feel affection for me?" even as
she's putting brown arm around my tense big neck.—
"Naturally baby."—"But what is the—?" I want to ask
everything, can't, don't know how, what is the mystery of
what I want from you, what is man or woman, love, what
do I mean by love or why do I have to insist and ask and
why do I go and leave you because in your poor wretched
little quarters—"It's the place depresses me—at home I sit
in the yard, under trees, feed my cat."—"Oh man I know
it's stuffy in here—shall I open the blind?"—"No everybody'll see you—I'll be so glad when the summer's over—
when I get that dough and we go to Mexico."—"Well
man, let's like you say go now on your money that you
have now, you say we can really make it."—"Okay! Okay!"
an idea which gains power in my brain as I take a few
swigs of stale beer and consider a dobe hut say outside
Texcoco at five dollars a month and we go to the market
in the early dewy morning she in her sweet brown feet
on sandals padding wifelike Ruthlike to follow me, we
come, buy oranges, load up on bread, even wine, local
wine, we go home and cook it up cleanly on our little
cooker, we sit together over coffee writing down our
dreams, analyzing them, we make love on our little bed.
—Now Mardou and I are sitting there talking all this
over, daydreaming, a big phantasy—"Well man," with
little teeth outlaughing, "WHEN do we do this—like it's

been a minor flip our whole relationship, all this inde-
cisive clouds and planning—God."—"Maybe we should
wait till I get that royalty dough—yep! really! it'll be better, cause like that we can get a typewriter and a three-
speed machine and Gerry Mulligan records and clothes
for you and everything we need, like the way it is now
we can't do anything."—"Yeah—I dunno" (brooding)
"Man you know I don't have any eyes for that hysterical
poverty deal"—(statements of such sudden pith and hip
I get mad and go home and brood about it for days).
"When will you be back?"—"Well okay, then we'll make
it Thursday."—"But if you really want to make it Friday
—don't let me interfere with your work, baby—maybe
you'd like it better to be away longer times."—"After what
you—O I love you—you—." I undress and stay another three
hours, and leave guiltily because the wellbeing, the sense
of doing what I should has been sacrificed, but tho sacrificed to healthy love, something is sick in me, lost, fears—
I realize too I have not given Mardou a dime, a loaf of
bread literally, but talk, hugs, kisses, I leave the house
and her unemployment check hasn't come and she has
nothing to eat—"What will you eat?"—"O there's some
cans—or I can go to Adam's maybe—but I don't wanta go
there too often—I feel he resents me now, your friendship
has been, I've come between that certain something you
had sort of—." "No you didn't."—"But it's something else
—I don't want to go out, I want to stay in, see no one"—
"Not even me?"—"Not even you, sometimes God I feel

[56]

that."—"Ah Mardou, I'm all mixed up—I can't make up my mind—we ought to do something together—I know what, I'll get a job on the railroad and we'll live together—" this is the great new idea.

(And Charles Bernard, the vastness of the name in the cosmogony of my brain, a hero of the Proustian past in the scheme as I knew it, in the Frisco-alone branch of it, Charles Bernard who'd been Jane's lover, Jane who'd been shot by Frank, Jane whom I'd lived with, Marie's best friend, the cold winter rainy nights when Charles would be crossing the campus saying something witty, the great epics almost here sounding phantom like and uninteresting if at all believable but the true position and bigburn importance of not only Charles but a good dozen others in the light rack of my brain, so Mardou seen in this light, is a little brown body in a gray sheet bed in the slums of Telegraph Hill, huge figure in the history of the night yes but only one among many, the asexuality of the WORK—also the sudden gut joy of beer when the visions of great words in rhythmic order all in one giant archangel book go roaring thru my brain, so I lie in the dark also seeing also hearing the jargon of the future worlds—damajehe eleout ekeke dhdkdk dldoud, ————d, ekeoeu dhdhdkehgyt—better not a more than lther ehe the macmurphy out of that dgardent that which strangely he doth mdodudltkdip—baseeaatra—poor examples because of mechanical needs of typing, of the flow of river sounds, words, dark, leading to the future and attesting to the madness, hollowness, ring and roar of my mind which blessed or unblessed is where trees sing—in a funny wind—well-being believes he'll go to heaven—a word to the wise is enough—"Smart went Crazy," wrote Allen Ginsberg.)

Reason why I didn't go home at 3 A.M.—and example.

AT FIRST I had doubts, because she was Negro, because she was sloppy (always putting off everything till tomorrow, the dirty room, unwashed sheets—what do I really for Christ's sake care about sheets)—doubts because I knew she'd been seriously insane and could very well be again and one of the first things we did, the first nights, she was going into the bathroom

naked in the abandoned hall but the door of her place
having a strange squeak it sounded to me (high on tea)
like suddenly someone had come up and was standing
in the stairwell (like maybe Gonzalez the Mexican sort
of bum or hanger-on sort of faggish who kept coming up
to her place on the strength of some old friendship she'd
had with some Tracy Pachucos to bum little 7 centses
from her or two cigarettes and all the time usually when
she was at her lowest, sometime even to take negotiable
bottles away), thinking it might be him, or some of the
subterraneans, in the hall asking "Is anybody with you?"
and she naked, unconcernedly, and like in the alley just
stands there saying, "No man, you better come back
tomorrow I'm busy I'm not alone," this my tea-revery as I
lay there, because the moansqueak of the door had that
moan of voices in it, so when she got back from the
toilet I told her this (reasoning honesty anyway) (and
believing it had been really so, almost, and still believing
her actively insane, as on the fence in the alley) but when
she heard my confession she said she almost flipped again
and was frightened of me and almost got up and ran out
—for reasons like this, madness, repeated chances of more
madness, I had my "doubts" my male self-contained
doubts about her, so reasoned, "I'll just as some time cut
out and get me another girl, white, white thighs, etc., and
it'll have been a grand affair and I hope I don't hurt her
tho."—Ha!—doubts because she cooked sloppily and never
cleaned up dishes right away, which at first I didn't like

and then came to see she really didn't cook sloppily and did wash the dishes after awhile and at the age of six (she later told me) she was forced to wash dishes for her tyrannical uncle's family and all the time on top of that forced to go out in alley in dark night with garbage pan every night same time where she was convinced the same ghost lurked for her—doubts, doubts—which I have not now in the luxury of time-past.—What a luxury it is to know that now I want her forever to my breast my prize my own woman whom I would defend from all Yuries and anybodies with my fists and anything else, *her* time has come to claim independence, announcing, only yesterday ere I began this tearbook, "I want to be an independent chick with money and cuttin' around."— Yeah, and knowing and screwing everybody, Wandering-foot," I'm thinking, wandering foot from when we—I'd stood at the bus stop in the cold wind and there were a lot of men there and instead of standing at my side she wandered off in little funny red raincoat and black slacks and went into a shoestore doorway (ALWAYS DO WHAT YOU WANT TO DO AIN'T NOTHIN' I LIKE BETTER THAN A GUY DOIN' WHAT HE WANTS, Leroy always said) so I follow her reluctantly thinking, "She sure has wandering feet to hell with her I'll get another chick" (weakening at this point as reader can tell from tone) but turns out she knew I had only shirt no undershirt and should stand where no wind was, telling me later, the realization that she did not talk naked to anyone in the hall any more than it was wandering-foot to walk away to lead me to a warmer waitingplace, that it was no more than shit, still making no impression on my eager impressionable ready-to-create construct destroy and die brain—as will be seen in the great construction of jealousy which I later from a dream and for reasons of self-laceration recreated. . . . Bear with me all lover readers who've suffered pangs, bear with me men who understand that the sea of blackness in a darkeyed woman's eyes is the lonely sea itself and would you go ask the sea to explain itself, or ask woman why she crosseth hands on lap over rose? no—

Doubts, therefore, of, well, Mardou's Negro, naturally not only my mother but my sister whom I may have to live with some day and her husband a Southerner and everybody concerned, would be mortified to hell and have nothing to do with us—like it would preclude completely the possibility of living in the South, like in that Faulk-nerian pillar homestead in the Old Granddad moonlight I'd so long envisoned for myself and there I am with Doctor Whitley pulling out the panel of my rolltop desk and we drink to great books and outside the cobwebs on the pines and old mules clop in soft roads, what would they say if my mansion lady wife was a black Cherokee, it would cut my life in half, and all such sundry awful American as if to say white ambition thoughts or white daydreams.—Doubts galore too about her body itself, again, and in a funny way really relaxing now to her love

so surprising myself I couldn't believe it, I'd seen it in
the light one playful night so I—walking through the
Fillmore she insisted we confess everything we'd been
hiding for this first week of our relationship, in order to
see and understand and I gave my first confession, halt-
ingly, "I thought I saw some kind of black thing I've
never seen before, hanging, like it *scared* me" (laughing)
—it must have stabbed her heart to hear, it seemed to me
I felt some kind of shock in her being at my side as she
walked as I divulged this secret thought—but later in the
house with light on we both of us childlike examined
said body and looked closely and it wasn't anything
pernicious and pizen juices but just bluedark as in all
kinds of women and I was really and truly reassured to
actually see and make the study with her—but this being
a doubt that, confessed, warmed her heart to me and
made her see that fundamentally I would never snakelike
hide the furthest, not the—but no need to defend, I
cannot at all possibly begin to understand who I am or
what I am any more, my love for Mardou has completely
separated me from any previous phantasies valuable and
otherwise—The thing therefore that kept these outburst
doubts from holding upper sway in my activity in relating
with her was the realization not only that she was sexy
and sweet and good for me and I was cutting quite a
figure with her on the Beach anyway (and in a sense too
now cutting the subterraneans who were becoming
progressively deeply colder in their looks towards me

in Dante's and on street from natural reasons that I had
taken over their play doll and one of their really if not
the most brilliant gals in their orbit)—Adam also saying,
"You go well together and it's good for you," he being
at the time and still my artistic and paternal manager—
not only this, but, hard to confess, to show how abstract
the life in the city of the Talking Class to which we all
belong, the Talking Class trying to rationalize itself I
suppose out of a really base almost lecherous lustful
materialism—it was the reading, the sudden illuminated
glad wondrous discovery of Wilhelm Reich, his book
The Function of the Orgasm, clarity as I had not seen in
a long time, not since perhaps the clarity of personal
modern grief of Céline, or, say, the clarity of Carmody's
mind in 1945 when I first sat at his feet, the clarity of
the poesy of Wolfe (at 19 it was clarity for me), the
clarity here tho was scientific, Germanic, beautiful, true
—something I'd always known and closely indeed connected to my 1948 sudden notion that the only thing that
really mattered was love, the lovers going to and fro beneath the boughs in the Forest of Arden of the World,
here magnified and at the same time microcosmed and
pointed in and maled into: orgasm—the reflexes of the
orgasm—you can't be healthy without normal sex love
and orgasm—I won't go into Reich's theory since it is
available in his own book—but at the same time Mardou
kept saying "O don't pull that Reich on me in bed, I read
his damn book, I don't want our relationship all pointed

out and f . . . . d up with what HE said," (and I'd
noticed that all the subterraneans and practically all
intellectuals I have known have really in the strangest
way always put down Reich if not at first, after awhile)
—besides which, Mardou did not gain orgasm from
normal copulation and only after awhile from stimula-
tion as applied by myself (an old trick that I had
learned with a previous frigid wife) so it wasn't so great
of me to make her come but as she finally only yesterday
said "You're doing this just to give me the pleasure of
coming, you're so kind," which was a statement suddenly
hard for either one of us to believe and came on the
heels of her "I think we ought to break up, we never do
anything together, and I want to be indep—" and so
doubts I had of Mardou, that I the great Finn Macpossipy
should take her for my long love wife here there or anywhere and with all the objections my family, especially
my really but sweetly but nevertheless really tyrannical
(because of my subjective view of her and her influence)
mother's sway over me—sway or whatever.—"Leo, I don't
think it's good for you to live with your mother always,"
Mardou, a statement that in my early confidence only
made me think, "Well naturally she, she's just jealous,
and has no folks herself, and is one of those modern
psychoanalyzed people who hate mothers anyway"—out
loud saying, "I really do really love her and love you too
and don't you see how hard I try to spend my time,
divide my time between the two of you—over there it's

my writing work, my well-being and when she comes home from work at night, tired, from the store, mind you, I feel very good making her supper, having the supper and a martini ready when she walks in so by 8 o'clock the dishes are all cleared, see, and she has more time to look at her television—which I worked on the railroad six months to buy her, see."—"Well you've done a lot of things for her," and Adam Moorad (whom my mother considered mad and evil) too had once said "You've really done a lot for her, Leo, forget her for a while, you've got your own life to live," which is exactly what my mother always was telling me in the dark of the South San Francisco night when we relaxed with Tom Collinses under the moon and neighbors would join us, "You have your own life to live, I won't interfere, Ti Leo, with anything you want to do, you decide, of course it will be all right with me," me sitting there goopy realizing it's all myself, a big subjective phantasy that my mother really needs me and would die if I weren't around, and nevertheless having a bellyful of other rationalizations allowing me to rush off two or three times a year on gigantic voyages to Mexico or New York or Panama Canal on ships—A million doubts of Mardou, now dispelled, now (and even without the help of Reich who shows life is simply the man entering the woman and the rubbing of the two in soft—that essence, that dingdong essence—something making me now almost so mad as to shout, I GOT MY OWN LITTLE BANGTAIL ESSENCE AND

THAT ESSENCE IS MIND RECOGNITION—) now no more doubts. Even, a thousand times, I without even remembering later asked her if she'd really stolen the pornographic picture from Bernard and the last time finally she fired "But I've told you and told you, about eight times in all, I did not take that picture and I told you too a thousand times I don't even didn't even have any pockets whatever in that particular suit I was wearing that night—no pockets at all," yet it never making an impression (in feverish folly brain me) that it was Bernard now who was really crazy, Bernard had gotten older and developed some personal sad foible, accusing others of stealing, solemnly—"Leo don't you see and you keep asking it"—this being the last deepest final doubt I wanted about Mardou that she was really a thief of some sort and therefore was out to steal my heart, my white man heart, a Negress sneaking in the world sneaking the holy white men for sacrificial rituals later when they'll be roasted and roiled (remembering the Tennessee Williams story about the Negro Turkish bath attendant and the little white fag) because, not only Ross Wallenstein had called me to my face a fag—"Man what are you, a fag? you talk you just like a fag," saying this after I'd said to him in what I hoped were cultured tones, "You're on goofballs tonight? you ought to try three sometimes, they'll really knock you out and have a few beers too, but don't take four, just three," it insulting him completely since he is the veteran hipster of the Beach and for

anyone especially a brash newcomer stealing Mardou
from his group and at the same time hoodlum-looking
with a reputation as a great writer, which he didn't
see, from only published book—the whole mess of it,
Mardou becoming the big buck nigger Turkish bath
attendant, and I the little fag who's broken to bits in the
love affair and carried to the bay in a burlap bag, there
to be distributed piece by piece and broken bone by bone
to the fish if there are still fish in that sad water)—so she'd
thieve my soul and eat it—so told me a thousand times,
"I did not steal that picture and I'm sure Aylward whats-
hisname didn't and you didn't it's just Bernard, he's got
some kind of fetish there"—But it never impressed and
stayed till the last, only the other night, time—that deepest doubt about her arising too from the time, (which
she'd told me about) she was living in Jack Steen's pad
in a crazy loft down on Commercial Street near the
seamen's union halls, in the glooms, had sat in front of
his suitcase an hour thinking whether she ought to look
in it to see what he had there, then Jack came home and
rummaged in it and thought or saw something was missing and said, sinister, sullen, "Have you been going thru
my bag?" and she almost leaped up and cried YES because she HAD—"Man I had, in Mind, been going thru
that bag all day and suddenly he was looking at me, with
that look—I almost flipped"—that story also not impressing
into my rigid paranoia-ridden brain, so for two months
I went around thinking she'd told me, "Yes, I did go thru

his bag but of course took nothing," but so I saw she'd lied to Jack Steen in reality—but in reality now, the facts, she had only thought to do so, and so on—my doubts all of them hastily ably assisted by a driving paranoia, which is really my confession—doubts, then, all gone.

For now I want Mardou—she just told me that six months ago a disease took root deeply in her soul, and forever now—doesn't this make her more beautiful?— But I want Mardou—because I see her standing, with her black velvet slacks, handsapockets, thin, slouched, cig hanging from lips, the smoke itself curling up, her little black hairs of short haircut combed down fine and sleek, her lipstick, pale brown skin, dark eyes, the way shadows play on her high cheekbones, the nose, the little soft shape of chin to neck, the little Adam's apple, so hip, so cool, so beautiful, so modern, so new, so unattainable to sad bagpants me in my shack in the middle of the woods—I want her because of the way she imitated Jack Steen that time on the street and it amazed me so much but Adam Moorad was solemn watching the imitation as if perhaps engrossed in the thing itself, or just skeptical, but she disengaged herself from the two men she was walking with and went ahead of them showing the walk (among crowds) the soft swing of arms, the long cool strides, the stop on the corner to hang and softly face up to birds with like as I say Viennese philosopher—but to see her do it, and to a T, (as I'd seen his walk indeed across the park), the fact of her—I love

her but this song is . . . broken—but in French now . . .
in French I can sing her on and on. . . .

Our little pleasures at home at night, she eats an
orange, she makes a lot of noise sucking it—

When I laugh she looks at me with little round black
eyes that hide themselves in her lids because she laughs
hard (contorting all her face, showing the little teeth,
making lights everywhere) (the first time I saw her, at
Larry O'Hara's, in the corner, I remember, I'd put my
face close to hers to talk about books, she'd turned her
face to me close, it was an ocean of melting things and
drowning, I could have swimmed in it, I was afraid of
all that richness and looked away)—

With her rose bandana she always puts on for the
pleasures of the bed, like a gypsy, rose, and then later
the purple one, and the little hairs falling black from the
phosphorescent purple in her brow as brown as wood—

Her little eyes moving like cats—

We play Gerry Mulligan loud when he arrives in the
night, she listens and chews her fingernails, her head
moves slowly side to side like a nun in profound prayer—

When she smokes she raises the cigarette to her mouth
and slits her eyes—

She reads till gray dawn, head on one arm, *Don
Quixote*, Proust, anything—

We lie down, look at each other seriously saying nothing, head to head on the pillow—

Sometimes when she speaks and I have my head under

hers on the pillow and I see her jaw the dimple the woman in her neck, I see her deeply, richly, the neck, the deep chin, I know she's one of the most *enwomaned* women I've seen, a brunette of eternity incomprehensibly beautiful and for always sad, profound, calm—

When I catch her in the house, small, squeeze her, she yells out, tickles me furiously, I laugh, she laughs, her eyes shine, she punches me, she wants to beat me with a switch, she says she likes me—

I'm hiding with her in the secret house of the night—

Dawn finds us mystical in our shrouds, heart to heart—

"My sister!" I'd thought suddenly the first time I saw her—

The light is out.

Daydreams of she and I bowing at big fellaheen cocktail parties somehow with glittering Parises in the horizon and in the forefront—she's crossing the long planks of my floor with a smile.

Always putting her to a test, which goes with "doubts" —doubts indeed—and I would like to accuse myself of bastardliness—such tests—briefly I can name two, the night Arial Lavalina the famous young writer suddenly was standing in the Mask and I was sitting with Carmody also now famous writer in a way who'd just arrived from North Africa, Mardou around the corner in Dante's cutting back and forth as was our wont all around, from bar to bar, and sometimes she'd cut unescorted there to see the Juliens and others—I saw Lavalina and called his

name and he came over.—When Mardou came to get me
to go home I wouldn't go, I kept insisting it was an important literary moment, the meeting of those two
(Carmody having plotted with me a year earlier in dark
Mexico when we'd lived poor and beat and he's a junky,
"Write a letter to Ralph Lowry find out how I can get
to meet this here good-looking Arial Lavalina, man, look
at that picture on the back of *Recognition of Rome*,
ain't that something?" my sympathies with him in the
matter being personal and again like Bernard also queer
he was connected with the legend of the bigbrain of myself which was my WORK, that all consuming work, so
wrote the letter and all that) but now suddenly (after of
course no reply from the Ischia and otherwise grapevines
and certainly just as well for me at least) he was standing there and I recognized him from the night I'd met
him at the Met ballet when in New York in tux I'd cut
out with tuxed editor to see glitter nightworld New York
of letters and wit, and Leon Danillian, so I yelled "Arial
Lavalina! come here!" which he did.—When Mardou
came I said whispering gleefully "This is Arial Lavalina
ain't that mad!"—"Yeh man but I want to go home."—
And in those days her love meaning no more to me than
that I had a nice convenient dog chasing after me (much
like in my real secretive Mexican vision of her following
me down dark dobe streets of slums of Mexico City not
walking with me but following, like Indian woman) I
just goofed and said "But wait, you go home and wait

or me, I want to dig Arial and then I'll be home."—"But baby you said that the other night and you were two hours late and you don't know what pain it caused me to wait." (Pain!)—"I know but look," and so I took her around the block to persuade her, and drunk as usual at one point to prove something I stood on my head in the pavement of Montgomery or Clay Street and some hoodlums passed by, saw this, saying "That's right"—finally (she laughing) depositing her in a cab, to get home, wait for me—going back to Lavalina and Carmody whom gleefully and now alone back in my big world night adolescent literary vision of the world, with nose pressed to window glass, "Will you look at that, Carmody and Lavalina, the great Arial Lavalina tho not a great great writer like me nevertheless so famous and glamorous etc. together in the Mask and I arranged it and everything ties together, the myth of the rainy night, Master Mad, Raw Road, going back to 1949 and 1950 and all things grand great the Mask of old history crusts"—(this my feeling and I go in) and sit with them and drink further—repairing the three of us to 13 Pater a lesbian joint down Columbus, Carmody, high, leaving us to go enjoy it, and we sitting in there, further beers, the horror the unspeakable horror of myself suddenly finding in myself a kind of perhaps William Blake or Crazy Jane or really Christopher Smart alcoholic humility grabbing and kissing Arial's hand and exclaiming "Oh Arial you dear—you are going to be—you are so famous—you wrote

so well— I remember you—what—" whatever and now
unrememberable and drunkenness, and there he is a
well-known and perfectly obvious homosexual of the first
water, my roaring brain— we go to his suite in some
hotel—I wake up in the morning on the couch, filled
with the first horrible recognition, "I didn't go back to
Mardou's at all" so in the cab he gives me—I ask for
fifty cents but he gives me a dollar saying "You owe me
a dollar" and I rush out and walk fast in the hot sun face
all broken from drinking and chagrin to her place down
in Heavenly Lane arriving just as she's dressing up to
go to the therapist.—Ah sad Mardou with little dark eyes
looking with pain and had waited all night in a dark
bed and the drunken man leering in and I rushed down
in fact at once to get two cans of beer to straighten up
("To curb the fearful hounds of hair" Old Bull Balloon
would say), so as she abluted to go out I yelled and
cavorted—went to sleep, to wait for her return, which
was in the late afternoon, waking to hear the cry of pure
children in the alleyways down there—the horror the
horror, and deciding, "I'll write a letter at once to
Lavalina," enclosing a dollar and apologizing for getting
so drunk and acting in such a way as to mislead him—
Mardou returning, no complaints, only a few a little later,
and the days rolling and passing and still she forgives me
enough or is humble enough in the wake of my crashing
star in fact to write me, a few nights later, this letter:

Jack Kerouac

DEAR BABY,
Isn't it good to know winter
is coming—

as we'd been complaining so much about heat and now
the heat was ended, a coolness came into the air, you
could feel it in the draining gray airshaft of Heavenly
Lane and in the look of the sky and nights with a greater
wavy glitter in streetlights—

> *—and that life will be a little more quiet—and*
> *you will be home writing and eating well and*
> *we will be spending pleasant nights wrapped*
> *round one another—and you are home now,*
> *rested and eating well because you should not*
> *become too sad—*

written after, one night, in the Mask with her and newly
arrived and future enemy Yuri erstwhile close lil brother
I'd suddenly said "I feel impossibly sad and like I'll die,
what can we do?" and Yuri'd suggested "Call Sam,"
which, in my sadness, I did, and so earnestly, as otherwise he'd pay no attention being a newspaper man and
new father and no time to goof, but so earnestly he
accepted us, the three, to come at once, from the Mask,
to his apartment on Russian Hill, where we went, I
getting drunker than ever, Sam as ever punching me and
saying "The trouble with you, Percepied," and, "You've

got rotten bags in the bottom of your store," and, "You
Canucks are really all alike and I don't even believe
you'll admit it when you die"—Mardou watching amused,
drinking a little, Sam finally, as always falling over
drunk, but not really, drunk-desiring, over a little low-
table covered a foot high with ashtrays piled three inches
high and drinks and doodads, crash, his wife, with baby
just from crib, sighing—Yuri, who didn't drink but only
watched bead-eyed, after having said to me the first day
of his arrival, "You know Percepied I really like you now,
I really feel like communicating with you now," which
I should have suspected, in him, as constituting a new
kind of sinister interest in the innocence of my activities,
that being by the name of, Mardou—

—because you should not become too sad

was only sweet comment heartbreakable Mardou made
about that disastrous awful night—similar to example
2, one following the one with Lavalina, the night of the
beautiful faun boy who'd been in bed with Micky two
years before at a great depraved wildparty I'd myself
arranged in days when living with Micky the great doll
of the roaring legend night, seeing him in the Mask, and
being with Frank Carmody and everybody, tugging at
his shirt, insisting he follow us to other bars, follow us
around, Mardou finally in the blur and roar of the night
yelling at me "It's him or me goddamit," but not really
serious (herself usually not a drinker because a subter-

ranean but in her affair with Percepied a big drinker
now)—she left, I heard her say "We're through" but
never for a moment believed it and it was not so, she
came back later, I saw her again, we swayed together,
once more I'd been a bad boy and again ludicrously like
a fag, this distressing me again in waking in gray
Heavenly Lane in the morning beer roared.—This is the
confession of a man who can't drink.—And so her letter
saying:

> *because you should not become too sad—and I*
> *feel better when you are well—*

forgiving, forgetting all this sad folly when all she wants
to do, "I don't want to go out drinking and getting drunk
with all your friends and keep going to Dante's and see
all those Juliens and everybody again, I want us to stay
quiet at home, listen to KPFA and read or something,
or go to a show, baby I like shows, movies on Market
Street, I really do."—"But I hate movies, life's more
interesting!" (another putdown)—her sweet letter con-
tinuing:

> *I am full of strange feelings, reliving and re-*
> *fashioning many old things*

—when she was 14 or 13 maybe she'd play hooky from
school in Oakland and take the ferry to Market Street
and spend all day in one movie, wandering around hav-

ing hallucinated phantasies, looking at all the eyes, a little Negro girl roaming the shuffle restless street of winos, hoodlums, sams, cops, paper peddlers, the mad mixup there the crowd eyeing looking everywhere the sexfiend crowd and all of it in the gray rain of hooky days—poor Mardou—"I'd get sexual phantasies the strangest kind, not with like sex acts with people but strange situations that I'd spend all day working out as I walked, and my orgasms the few I had only came, because I never masturbated or even knew how, when I dreamed that my father or somebody was leaving me, running away from me, I'd wake up with a funny convulsion and wetness in myself, in my thighs, and on Market Street the same way but different and anxiety dreams woven out of the movies I saw."—Me thinking *O grayscreen gangster cocktail rainyday roaring gunshot spectral immortality B movie tire pile black-in-the-mist Wildamerica but it's a crazy world!*—"Honey" (out loud) "wished I could have seen you walking around Market like that—I bet I DID see you—I bet I did— you were thirteen and I was twenty-two—1944, yeah I bet I saw you, I was a seaman, I was always there, I knew the gangs around the bars—" So in her letter saying:

reliving and refashioning many old things

probably reliving those days and phantasies, and earlier cruder horrors of home in Oakland where her aunt hysterically beat her or hysterically tried and her sisters (tho occasional littlesister tenderness like dutiful kisses before bed and writing on one another's backs) giving her a bad time, and she roaming the street late, deep in broodthoughts and men trying to make her, the dark men of dark colored-district doors—so going on,

> *and feeling the cold and the quietude even in the midst of my forebodings and fears—which clear nights soothe and make more sharp and real—tangible and easier to cope with*

—said indeed with a nice rhythm, too, so I remember admiring her intelligence even then—but at the same time darkening at home there at my desk of well-being and thinking, "But cope that old psychoanalytic cope, she talks like all of em, the city decadent intellectual dead-ended in cause-and-effect analysis and solution of so-called problems instead of the great JOY of being and will and fearlessness—rupture's their rapture—that's her trouble, she's just like Adam, like Julien, the lot, afraid of madness, the fear of madness haunts her—not Me Not Me by God"—

> *But why am I writing to say these things to you. But all feelings are real and you probably discern or feel too what I am saying and why I need to write it—*

—a sentiment of mystery and charm—but, as I told her often, not enough detail, the details are the life of it, I insist, say everything on your mind, don't hold it back, don't analyze or anything as you go along, say it out, "That's" (I now say in reading letter) "a typical example —but no mind, she's just a girl—humph"—

My image of you now is strange

—I see the bough of that statement, it waves on the tree—

I feel a distance from you which you might feel too which gives me a picture of you that is warm and friendly

and then inserts, in smaller writing,

(and loving)

to obviate my feeling depressed probably over seeing in a letter from lover only word "friendly"—but that whole complicated phrase further complicated by the fact it is presented in originally written form under the marks and additions of a rewrite, which is not as interesting to me, naturally—the rewrite being

I feel a distance from you which you might feel too with pictures of you that are warm and friendly (and loving)

—and because of the anxieties we are experi-
encing but never speak of really, and are similar
too—

a piece of communication making me suddenly by some
majesty of her pen feel sorry for myself, seeing myself
like her lost in the suffering ignorant sea of human life
feeling distant from she who should be closest and not
knowing (no not under the sun) why the distance instead
is the feeling, the both of us entwined and lost in that,
as under the sea—

I am going to sleep to dream, to wake

—hints of our business of writing down dreams or telling
dreams on waking, all the strange dreams indeed and
(later will show) the further brain communicating we
did, telepathizing images together with eyes closed,
where it will be shown, all thoughts meet in the crystal
chandelier of eternity—Jim—yet I also like the rhythm
of *to dream, to wake,* and flatter myself I have a rhythmic
girl in any case, at my metaphysical homedesk—

You have a very beautiful face and I like to see
it as I do now—

—echoes of that New York girl's statement and now
coming from humble meek Mardou not so unbelievable
and I actually begin to preen and believe in this (O

humble paper of letters, O the time I sat on a log near
Idlewild airport in New York and watched the helicopter
flying in with the mail and as I looked I saw the smile
of all the angels of earth who'd written the letters which
were packed in its hold, the smiles of them, specifically
of my mother, bending over sweet paper and pen to
communicate by mail with her daughter, the angelical
smile like the smiles of workingwomen in factories, the
world-wide bliss of it and the courage and beauty of it,
recognition of which facts I shouldn't even deserve,
treating Mardou as I have done) (O forgive me angels
of the heaven and of the earth—even Ross Wallenstein
will go to heaven)—

Forgive the conjunctions and double infinitives
and the not said

—again I'm impressed and I think, she too there, for
the first time self-conscious of writing to an author—

I don't know really what I wanted to say but
want you to have a few words from me this
Wednesday morning

and the mail only carried it in much later, after I saw
her, the letter losing therefore its hopeful impactedness

We are like two animals escaping to dark warm
holes and live our pains alone

—at this time my dumb phantasy of the two of us (after all the drunks making me drunksick city sick) was, a shack in the middle of the Mississippi woods, Mardou with me, damn the lynchers, the not-likings, so I wrote back: "I hope you meant by that line (*animals to dark warm holes*) you'll turn out to be the woman who can really live with me in profound solitude of woods finally and at same time make the glittering Parises (there it is) and grow old with me in my cottage of peace" (suddenly seeing myself as William Blake with the meek wife in the middle of London early dewy morning, Crabbe Robinson is coming with some more etching work but Blake is lost in the vision of the Lamb at breakfast leavings table).—Ah regrettable Mardou, and never a thought of that thing beats in your brow, that I should kiss, the pain of your own pride, enough 19th-century romantic general talk—the details are the life of it—(a man may act stupid and top tippity and bigtime 19th-century boss type dominant with a woman but it won't help him when the chips are down—the loss lass'll make it back, it's hidden in her eyes, her future triumph and strength—on his lips we hear nothing but "of course love").—Her closing words a beautiful pastichepattisee, or pie, of—

Write to me anything Please Stay Well Your Freind [misspelled] *And my love And Oh* [over some kind of hiddenforever erasures] [and many X's for of course kisses] *And Love for You* MARDOU [underlined]

and weirdest, most strange, central of all—ringed by itself, the word, PLEASE—her lastplea neither one of us
knowing—Answering this letter myself with a dull boloney bullshit rising out of my anger with the incident of
the pushcart.

(And tonight this letter is my last hope.)

The incident of the pushcart began, again as usual, in
the Mask and Dante's, drinking, I'd come in to see
Mardou from my work, we were in a drinking mood,
for some reason suddenly I wanted to drink red Burgundy
wine which I'd tasted with Frank and Adam and Yuri the
Sunday before—another, and first, worthy of mention
incident, being—but that's the crux of it all—THE
DREAM. Oh the bloody dream! In which there was a
pushcart, and everything else prophesied. This too after
a night of severe drinking, the night of the redshirt faun
boy—where everybody afterward of course said "You
made a fool of yourself, Leo, you're making yourself a
reputation on the Beach as a big fag tugging at the shirts
of well-known punks."—"But I only wanted him for
you to dig."—"Nevertheless" (Adam) *really.*"—And
Frank: "You really makin a horrible reputation."—Me:
"I don't care, you remember 1948 when Sylvester Strauss
that fag composer got sore at me because I wouldn't go
to bed with him because he'd read my novel and sub-
mitted it, yelled at me 'I know all about you and your
awful reputation.'—'What?'—'You and that there Sam

Vedder go around the Beach picking up sailors and giving them dope and he makes them only so he can bite, I've heard about you.'— 'Where did you hear this fantastic tale?'—you know that story, Frank."—"I should imagine" (Frank laughing) "what with all the things you do right there in the Mask, drunk, in front of everybody, if I didn't know you I'd swear you were the craziest piece of rough trade that ever walked" (a typical Carmodian pithy statement) and Adam "Really that's true."—After the night of the redshirt boy, drunk, I'd slept with Mardou and had the worst nightmare of all, which was, everybody, the whole world was around our bed, we lay there and everything was happening. Dead Jane was there, had a big bottle of Tokay wine hidden in Mardou's dresser for me and got it out and poured me a big slug and spilled a lot out of the waterglass on the bed (a symbol of even further drinking, more wine, to come)— and Frank with her—and Adam, who went out the door to the dark tragic Italian pushcart Telegraph Hill street, going down the rickety wooden Shatov stairs where the subterraneans were "digging an old Jewish patriarch just arrived from Russia" who is holding some ritual by the barrels of the fish head cats (the fish heads, in the height of the hot days Mardou had a fish head for our crazy little visiting cat who was almost human in his insistence to be loved his scrolling of neck and purring to be against you, for him she had a fish head which smelled so horrible in the almost airless night I threw part of it out in

the barrel downstairs after first throwing a piece of slimy
gut unbeknownst I'd put my hands against in the dark
icebox where was a small piece of ice I wanted to chill
my sauterne with, smack against a great soft mass, the
guts or mouth of a fish, this being left in the icebox after
disposal of fish I threw it out, the piece draped over fire
escape and was there all hotnight and so in the morning
when waking I was being bitten by gigantic big blue
flies that had been attracted by the fish, I was naked and
they were biting like mad, which annoyed me, as the
pieces of pillow had annoyed me and somehow I tied it
up with Mardou's Indianness, the fish heads the awful
sloppy way to dispose of fish, she sensing my annoyance
but laughing, ah bird)—that alley, out there, in the
dream, Adam, and in the house, the actual room and bed
of Mardou and I the whole world roaring around us,
back ass flat—Yuri also there, and when I turn my head
(after nameless events of the millionfold mothswarms)
suddenly he's got Mardou on the bed laid out and wig-
gling and is necking furiously with her—at first I say
nothing—when I look again, again they're at it, I get mad
—I'm beginning to wake up, just as I give Mardou a
rabbit punch in the back of her neck, which causes Yuri
to reach a hand for me—I wake up I'm swinging Yuri by
the heels against the brick fireplace wall.—On waking
from this dream I told all to Mardou except the part
where I hit her or Yuri—and she too (in tying in with
our telepathies already experienced that sad summer

season now autumn mooned to death, we'd communi-
cated many feelings of empathy and I'd come running to
see her on nights when she sensed it) had been dreaming like me of the whole world around our bed, of
Frank, Adam, others, her recurrent dream of her father
rushing off, in a train, the spasm of almost orgasm.—"Ah
honey I want to stop all this drinking these nightmares'll
kill me—you don't know how jealous I was in that dream"
(a feeling I'd not yet had about Mardou)—the energy
behind this anxious dream had obtained from her reaction to my foolishness with the redshirt boy ("Absolutely
insufferable type anyway" Carmody had commented
"tho obviously good-looking, really Leo you were funny"
and Mardou: "Acting like a little boy but I like it.")—
Her reaction had of course been violent, on arriving
home, after she'd tugged me in the Mask in front of
everyone including her Berkeley friends who saw her
and probably even heard "It's me or him!" and the
madness humor futility of that—arriving in Heavenly
Lane she'd found a balloon in the hall, nice young writer
John Golz who lived downstairs had been playing bal-
loons with the kids of the Lane all day and some were
in the hall, with the balloon Mardou had (drunk) danced
around the floor, puffing and poooshing and flupping it
up with dance interpretive gestures and said something
that not only made me fear her madness, her hospital
type insanity, but cut my heart deeply, and so deeply
that she could not therefore have been insane, in com-

municating something so exactly, with precise—whatever —"You can go now I have this balloon."—"What do you mean?" (I, drunk, on floor blearing).—"I have this balloon now—I don't need you any more—goodbye—goo away—leave me alone"—a statement that even in my drunkenness made me heavy as lead and I lay there, on the floor, where I slept an hour while she played with the balloon and finally went to bed, waking me up at dawn to undress and get in—both of us dreaming the nightmare of the world around our bed—and that GUILT-Jealousy entering into my mind for the first time—the crux of this entire tale being: I want Mardou because she has begun to reject me—BECAUSE—"But baby that was a mad dream."—"I was so jealous—I was sick."—I hearkened suddenly now to what Mardou'd said the first week of our relationship, when, I thought secretly, in my mind I had privately superseded her importance with the importance of my writing work, as, in every romance, the first week is so intense all previous worlds are eligible for throwover, but when the energy (of mystery, pride) begins to wane, elder worlds of sanity, well-being, common sense, etc., return, so I had secretly told myself: "My work's more important than Mardou."—Nevertheless she'd sensed it, that first week, and now said, "Leo there's something different now— in you—I feel it in me—I don't know what it is." I knew very well what it was and pretended not to be able to articulate with myself and least of all with her anyway

—I remembered now, in the waking from the jealousy nightmare, where she necks with Yuri, something had changed, I could sense it, something in me was cracked, there was a new loss, a new Mardou even—and, again, the difference was not isolated in myself who had dreamed the cuckold dream, but in she, the subject, who'd not dreamed it, but participated somehow in the general rueful mixed up dream of all this life with me—so I felt she could now this morning look at me and tell that something had died—not due to the balloon and "You can go now"—but the dream—and so the dream, the dream, I kept harping on it, desperately I kept chewing and telling about it, over coffee, to her, finally when Carmody and Adam and Yuri came (in themselves lonely and looking to come get juices from that great current between Mardou and me running, a current everybody I found out later wanted to get in on, the act) I began telling *them* about the dream, stressing, stressing, stressing the Yuri part, where Yuri "every time I turn my back" is kissing her—naturally the others wanting to know their parts, which I told with less vigor—a sad Sunday afternoon, Yuri going out to get beer, a spread, bread—eating a little—and in fact a few wrestling matches that broke my heart. For when I saw Mardou for fun wrestling with Adam (who was not the villain of the dream tho now I figured I must have switched persons) I was pierced with that pain that's now all over me, that firstpain, how cute she looked in her jeans wrestling

and struggling (I'd said "She's strong as hell, d'jever hear
of her fight with Jack Steen? try her Adam")—Adam
having already started to wrestle with Frank on some
impetus from some talk about holds, now Adam had
her pinned in the coitus position on the floor (which in
itself didn't hurt me)—it was her beautifulness, her game
guts wrestling, I felt proud, I wanted to know how
Carmody felt NOW (feeling he must have been at the
outset critical of her for being a Negro, he being a Texan
and a Texas gentleman-type at that) to see her be so
great, buddy like, joining in, humble and meek too and
a real woman. Even somehow the presence of Yuri, whose
personality was energized already in my mind from the
energy of the dream, added to my love of Mardou—I
suddenly loved her.—They wanted me to go with them,
sit in the park—as agreed in solemn sober conclaves
Mardou said "But I'll stay here and read and do things,
Leo, you go with them like we said"—as they left and
trooped down the stairs I stayed behind to tell her I
loved her now—she was not as surprised, or pleased, as
I wished—she had looked at Yuri now already with the
point of view eyes not only of my dream but had seen
him in a new light as a possible successor to me because
of my continual betrayal and getting drunk.

Yuri Gligoric: a young poet, 22, had just come down
from apple-picking Oregon, before that a waiter in a
big dude ranch dininghall—tall thin blond Yugoslavian,
good-looking, very brash and above all trying to cut

Adam and myself and Carmody, all the time knowing us as an old revered trinity, wanting, naturally, as a young unpublished unknown but very genius poet to destroy the big established gods and raise himself—wanting therefore their women too, being uninhibited, or unsaddened, yet, at least.—I liked him, considered him another new "young brother" (as Leroy and Adam before, whom I'd "shown" writing tricks) and now I would show Yuri and he would be a buddy with me and walk around with me and Mardou—his own lover, June, had left him, he'd treated her badly, he wanted her back, she was with another life in Compton, I sympathized with him and asked about the progress of his letters and phonecalls to Compton, and, most important, as I say he was now for the first time suddenly looking at me and saying "Percepied I want to talk to you—suddenly I want to really know you."—In a joke at the Sunday wine in Dante's I'd said "Frank's leching after Adam, Adam's leching after Yuri" and Yuri'd thrown in "And I'm leching after you."

Indeed he was indeed. On this mournful Sunday of my first pained love of Mardou after sitting in the park with the boys as agreed, I dragged myself again home, to work, to Sunday dinner, guiltily, arriving late, finding my mother glum and all-weekend-alone in a chair with her shawl . . . and my thoughts rich on Mardou now—not thinking it of any importance whatever that I had told young Yuri not only "I dreamed you were necking with Mardou" but also, at a soda fountain enroute to the park when Adam wanted to call Sam and we all sat at counter waiting, with limeades, "Since I saw you last I've fallen in love with that girl," information which he received without comment and which I hope he still remembers, and of course does.

And so now brooding over her, valuing the precious good moments we'd had that heretofore I'd avoided thinking of, came the fact, ballooning in importance, the amazing fact she is the only girl I've ever known who could really understand bop and sing it, she'd said that first cuddly day of the redbulb at Adam's "While I was flipping I heard bop, on juke boxes and in the Red Drum and wherever I was happening to hear it, with an entirely new and different sense, which tho, I really can't describe."—"But what was it like?"—"But I can't describe it, it not only sent waves—went through me—I can't, like, *make* it, in telling it in words, you know? OO dee bee dee dee" singing a few notes, so cutely.—The night we walked swiftly down Larkin past the Blackhawk with Adam actually but he was following and listening, close head to head, singing wild choruses of jazz and bop, at times I'd phrase and she did perfect in fact interesting modern and advanced chords (like I'd never heard anywhere and which bore resemblance to Bartok modern chords but were hep wise to bop) and at other times she just did her chords as I did the bass fiddle, in the old great legend (again of the roaring high davenport amazing smash-afternoon which I expect no one to understand) before, I'd with Ossip Popper sung bop, made records, always taking the part of the bass fiddle thum thum to his phrasing (so much I see now like Billy Eckstine's bop phrasing)—the two of us arm in arm rushing longstrides down Market the hip old apple of the California Apple singing bop and well too—the glee of it, and coming after an awful party at Roger Walker's where (Adam's arrangement and my acquiescence) instead of a regular party were just boys and all queer including one Mexican younghustler and Mardou far from being nonplused enjoyed herself and talked—nevertheless of it all, rushing home to the Third Street bus singing gleeful—

The time we read Faulkner together, I read her *Spotted Horses*, out loud—when Mike Murphy came in she told him to sit and listen as I'd go on but then I was different and I couldn't read the same and stopped—but next day in her gloomy solitude Mardou sat down and read the entire Faulkner portable.

The time we went to a French movie on Larkin, the Vogue, saw *The Lower Depths*, held hands, smoked, felt close—tho out on Market Street she would not have me hold her arm for fear people of the street there would think her a hustler, which it would look like but I felt mad but let it go and we walked along, I wanted to go into a bar for a wine, she was afraid of all the behatted men ranged at the bar, now I saw her Negro fear of American society she was always talking about but

palpably in the streets which never gave me any concern
—tried to console her, show her she could do anything
with me, "In fact baby I'll be a famous man and you'll
be the dignified wife of a famous man so don't worry"
but she said "You don't understand" but her little girl-
like fear so cute, so edible, I let it go, we went home, to
tender love scenes together in our own and secret dark—

Fact, the time, one of those fine times when we, or
that is, I didn't drink and we spent the whole night together in bed, this time telling ghost stories, the tales of
Poe I could remember, then we made some up, and
finally we were making madhouse eyes at each other and
trying to frighten with round stares, she showed me how
one of her Market Street reveries had been that she was
a catatonic ("Tho then I didn't know what the word
meant, but like, I walked stiffly hang arming arms hanging and man not a soul dared to speak to me and some
were afraid to look, there I was walking along zombie-
like and just thirteen.") (Oh gleeful shnuff-fleeflue in
fluffle in her little lips, I see the outthrust teeth, I say
sternly, "Mardou you must get your teeth cleaned at
once, at that hospital there, the therapist, get a dentist
too—it's all free so do it—" because I see beginnings of
bad congestion at the corners of her pearlies which would
lead to decay)—and she makes the madwoman face at
me, the face rigid, the eyes shining shining shining like
the stars of heaven and far from being frightened I am
utterly amazed at the beauty of her and I say "And I also

see the earth in your eyes that's what I think of you, you
have a certain kind of beauty, not that I'm hung up on
the earth and Indians and all that and wanta harp all the
time about you and us, but I see in your eyes such warm
—but when you make the madwoman I don't see madness but glee glee—it's like the ragamuffin dusts in the
little kid's corner and he's asleep in his crib now and I
love you, rain'll fall on our eaves some day sweetheart"—
and we have just candlelight so the mad acts are funnier
and the ghost stories more chilling—the one about the—
but a lack, a lark, I go larking in the good things and
don't and do forget my pain—

Extending the eye business, the time we closed our
eyes (again not drinking because of broke, poverty
would have saved this romance) and I sent her messages,
"Are you ready," and I see the first thing in my black eye
world and ask her to describe it, amazing how we came
to the same thing, it was some rapport, I saw crystal
chandeliers and she saw white petals in a black bog
just after some melding of images as amazing as the accurate images I'd exchange with Carmody in Mexico—
Mardou and I both seeing the same thing, some madness
shape, some fountain, now by me forgotten and really
not important yet, come together in mutual descriptions
of it and joy and glee in this telepathic triumph of ours,
ending where our thoughts meet at the crystal white and
petals, the mystery—I see the gleeful hunger of her face
devouring the sight of mine, I could die, don't break

my heart radio with beautiful music, O world—the candlelight again, flickering, I'd bought a slue of candles in the
store, the corners of our room in darkness, her shadow
naked brown as she hurries to the sink—our use of the
sink—my fear of communicating WHITE images to her
in our telepathies for fear she'll be (in her fun) reminded
of our racial difference, at that time making me feel
guilty, now I realize it was one love's gentility on my part
—Lord.

The good ones—going up on the top of Nob Hill at
night with a fifth of Royal Chalice Tokay, sweet, rich,
potent, the lights of the city and of the bay beneath us,
the sad mystery—sitting on a bench there, lovers, loners
pass, we pass the bottle, talk—she tells all her little girlhood in Oakland.—It's like Paris—it's soft, the breeze
blows, the city may swelter but the hillers do fly—and
over the bay is Oakland (ah me Hart Crane Melville and
all ye assorted brother poets of the American night that
once I thought would be my sacrificial altar and now it
is but who's to care, know, and I lost love because of it—
drunkard, dullard, poet)—returning via Van Ness to
Aquatic Park beach, sitting in the sand, as I pass Mexicans
I feel that great hepness I'd been having all summer on
the street with Mardou my old dream of wanting to be
vital, alive like a Negro or an Indian or a Denver Jap
or a New York Puerto Rican come true, with her by my
side so young, sexy, slender, strange, hip, myself in
jeans and casual and both of us as if young (I say as if,

to my 31)—the cops telling us to leave the beach, a
lonely Negro passing us twice and staring—we walk
along the waterslap, she laughs to see the crazy figures
of reflected light of the moon dancing so bug-like in the
ululating cool smooth water of the night—we smell har-
bors, we dance—

The time I walked her in broad sweet dry Mexico
plateau-like or Arizona-like morning to her appointment
with therapist at the hospital, along the Embarcadero,
denying the bus, hand in hand—I proud, thinking, "In
Mexico she'll look just like this and not a soul'll know
I'm not an Indian by God and we'll go along"—and I
point out the purity and clarity of the clouds, "Just like
Mexico honey, O you'll love it" and we go up the busy
street to the big grimbrick hospital and I'm supposed to
be going home from there but she lingers, sad smile, love
smile, when I give in and agree to wait for her 20-
minute interview and her coming out she radiantly breaks
out glad and rushes to the gate which we've already
passed in her almost therapy-giving-up strolling-with-me
meandering, men—love—not for sale—my prize—posses-
sion—nobody gets it but gets a Sicilian line down his
middle—a German boot in the kisser, an axe Canuck—
I'll pin them wriggling poets to some London wall right
here, explained.—And as I wait for her to come out, I sit
on side of water, in Mexico-like gravel and grass and concrete blocks and take out sketchbooks and draw big
word pictures of the skyline and of the bay, putting in a

little mention of the great fact of the huge all-world with its infinite levels, from Standard Oil top down to waterslap at barges where old bargemen dream, the difference between men, the difference so vast between concerns of executives in skyscrapers and seadogs on harbor and psychoanalysts in stuffy offices in great grim buildings full of dead bodies in the morgue below and madwomen at windows, hoping thereby to instill in Mardou recognition of fact it's a big world and psychoanalysis is a small way to explain it since it only scratches the surface, which is, analysis, cause and effect, why instead of what—when she comes out I read it to her, not impressing her too much but she loves me, holds my hand as we cut down along Embarcadero towards her place and when I leave her at Third and Townsend train in warm clear afternoon she says "O I hate to see you go, I really miss you now."—"But I gotta be home in time to make the supper—and write—so honey I'll be back, tomorrow remember promptly at ten."—And tomorrow I arrive at midnight instead.

The time we had a shuddering come together and she said "I was lost suddenly" and she was lost with me tho not coming herself but frantic in my franticness (Reich's beclouding of the senses) and how she loved it—all our teachings in bed, I explain me to her, she explains her to me, we work, we wail, we bop—we throw clothes off and jump at each other (after always her little trip to the diaphragm sink and I have to wait holding softer and

making goofy remarks and she laughs and trickles water)
then here she comes padding to me across the Garden
of Eden, and I reach up and help her down to my side
on the soft bed, I pull her little body to me and it is
warm, her warm spot is hot, I kiss her brown breasts
both of them, I kiss her loveshoulders—she keeps with
her lips going "ps ps ps" little kiss sounds where actually
no contact is made with my face except when hap-
hazardly while doing something else I do move it against
her and her little ps ps kisses connect and are as sad and
soft as when they don't—it's her little litany of night—
and when she's sick and we're worried, then she takes
me on her, on her arm, on mine—she services the mad
unthinking beast—I spend long nights and many hours
making her, finally I have her, I pray for it to come, I
can hear her breathing harder, I hope against hope it's
time, a noise in the hall (or whoop of drunkards next
door) takes her mind off and she can't make it and
laughs—but when she does make it I hear her crying,
whimpering, the shuddering electrical female orgasm
makes her sound like a little girl crying, moaning in the
night, it lasts a good twenty seconds and when it's over
she moans, "O why can't it last longer," and, "O when
will I when you do?"—"Soon now I bet," I say, "you're
getting closer and closer"—sweating against her in the
warm sad Frisco with its damn old scows mooing on the
tide out there, voom, voooom, and stars flickering on
the water even where it waves beneath the pierhead

where you expect gangsters dropping encemented bodies, or rats, or The Shadow—my little Mardou whom I love, who'd never read my unpublished works but only the first novel, which has guts but has a dreary prose to it when all's said and done and so now holding her and spent with sex I dream of the day she'll read great works by me and admire me, remembering the time Adam had said in sudden strangeness in his kitchen, "Mardou, what do you really think of Leo and myself as writers, our positions in the world, the rack of time," asking her that, knowing that her thinking is in accord in some ways more or less with the subterraneans whom he admires and fears, whose opinions he values with wonder—Mardou not really replying but evading the issue, but old man me plots greatbooks for her amaze—all those good things, good times we had, others I am now in the heat of my frenzy forgetting but I must tell all, but angels know all and record it in books—

But think of all the bad times—I have a list of bad times to make the good times, the times I was good to her and like I should be, to make it sick—when early in our love I was three hours late which is a lot of hours of lateness for younglovers, and so she wigged, got frightened, walked around the church handsapockets brooding looking for me in the mist of dawn and I ran out (seeing her note saying "I am gone out to look for you") (in all Frisco yet! that east and west, north and south of soulless loveless bleak she'd seen from the fence, all the countless men in hats going into buses and not caring about the naked girl on the fence, why)—when I saw her, I myself running out to find her, I opened my arms a halfmile away—

The worst almost worst time of all when a red flame crossed my brain, I was sitting with her and Larry O'Hara in his pad, we'd been drinking French Bordeaux and blasting, a subject was up, I had a hand on Larry's knee shouting "But listen to me, but listen to me!" wanting to make my point so bad there was a big crazy plead in the tone and Larry deeply engrossed in what Mardou is saying simultaneously and feeding a few words to her dialog, in the emptiness after the red flame I suddenly leap up and rush to the door and tug at it, ugh, locked, the indoor chain lock, I slide and undo it and with another try I lunge out in the hall and down the stairs as fast as my thieves' quick crepesoul shoes'll take me, putt pitterpit, floor after floor reeling around me as I round the stairwell, leaving them agape up there—calling back in half hour, meeting her on the street three blocks away —there is no hope—

The time even when we'd agreed she needed money for food, that I'd go home and get it and just bring it back and stay a short while, but I'm at this time far from in love, but bugged, not only her pitiful demands for money but that doubt, that old Mardou-doubt, and so rush into her pad, Alice her friend is there, I use that as an excuse (because Alice dike-like silent unpleasant and strange and likes no one) to lay the two bills on Mardou's dishes at sink, kiss a quick peck in the malt of her ear, say "I'll be back tomorrow" and run right out again without even asking her opinion—as if the whore'd made me for two bucks and I was sore.

How clear the realization one is going mad—the mind has a silence, nothing happens in the physique, urine gathers in your loins, your ribs contract.

Bad time she asked me, "What does Adam really think of me, you never told me, I know he resents us together but—" and I told her substantially what Adam had told me, of which none should have been divulged to her for the sake of her peace of mind, "He said it was just a social question of his not now wanting to get hung up with you lovewise because you're Negro"—feeling again her telepathic little shock cross the room to me, it sunk deep, I question my motives for telling her this.

The time her cheerful little neighbor young writer John Golz came up (he dutifully eight hours a day types working on magazine stories, admirer of Hemingway, often feeds Mardou and is a nice Indiana boy and means no harm and certainly not a slinky snaky interesting sub-terranean but openfaced, jovial, plays with children in the court for God's sake)—came up to see Mardou, I was there alone (for some reason, Mardou at a bar with our accord arrangement, the night she went out with a Negro boy she didn't like too much but just for fun and told Adam she was doing it because she wanted to make it with a Negro boy again, which made me jealous, but Adam said "If I should if she should hear that you went out with a white girl to see if you could make it again she'd sure be flattered, Leo")—that night, I was at her place waiting, reading, young John Golz came in to borrow cigarettes and seeing I was alone wanted to talk literature—"Well I believe that the most important thing is selectivity," and I blew up and said "Ah don't give me all that high school stuff I've heard it and heard it long before you were born almost for krissakes and really now, say something interesting and new about writing"—putting him down, sullen, for reasons mainly of irritation and because he seemed harmless and therefore could be counted on tò be safe to yell at, which he was —putting him down, her friend, was not nice—no, the world's no fit place for this kind of activity, and what we gonna do, and where? when? wha wha wha, the baby bawls in the midnight boom.

Nor could it have been charming and helpful to her fears and anxieties to have me start out, at the outset of our romance, "kissing her down between the stems"— starting and then suddenly quitting so later in an un-guarded drinkingmoment she said, "You suddenly stopped as tho I was—" and the reason I stopped being in itself not as significant as the reason I did it at all, to secure her greater sexual interest, which once tied on with a bow knot, I could dally out of—the warm lovemouth of the woman, the womb, being the place for men who love, not . . . this immature drunkard and egomaniacal . . . this . . . knowing as I do from past experience and interior sense, you've got to fall down on your knees and beg the woman's permission, beg the woman's forgiveness for all your sins, protect her, support her, doing everything for her, die for her but for God's sake love her and love her all the way in and every way you can—yes psychoanalysis, I hear (fearing secretly the few times I had come into contact with the rough stubble-like quality of the pubic, which was Negroid and therefore a little rougher, tho not enough to make any difference, and the insides itself I should say the best, the richest, most fecund moist warm and full of hidden soft slidy mountains, also the pull and force of the muscles being so powerful she unknowing often vice-like closes over and makes a dam-up and hurt, tho this I only realized the other night, too late—). And so the final lingering physiological doubt I have that this contraction and greatstrength of womb, responsible I think now in retrospect for the time when Adam in his first encounter with her experienced piercing unsupportable screamingsudden pain, so he had to go to the doctor and have himself bandaged and all (and even later when Carmody arrived and made a local orgone accumulator out of a big old watercan and burlap and vegetative materials placing the nozzle of himself into the nozzle of the can to heal), I now wonder and suspect if our little chick didn't really intend to bust us in half, if Adam isn't thinking it's his

own fault and doesn't know, but she contracted mightily
there (the lesbian!) (always knew it) and busted him
and fixed him and couldn't do it to me but tried enough
till she threw me over a dead hulk that now I am
—psychoanalyst, I'm serious!

It's too much. Beginning, as I say with the pushcart
incident—the night we drank red wine at Dante's and
were in a drinking mood now both of us so disgusted—
Yuri came with us, Ross Wallenstein was in there and
maybe to show off to Mardou Yuri acted like a kid all
night and kept hitting Wallenstein on the back of his
head with little finger taps like goofing in a bar but
Wallenstein (who's always being beaten up by hoodlums
because of this) turned around a stiff death's-head gaze
with big eyes glaring behind glasses, his Christlike blue
unshaven cheeks, staring rigidly as tho the stare itself will
floor Yuri, not speaking for a long time, finally saying,
"Man, don't bug me," and turning back to his conversation with friends and Yuri does it again and Ross turns
again the same pitiless awful subterranean sort of non-
violent Indian Mahatma Gandhi defense of some kind
(which I'd suspected that first time he talked to me
saying, "Are you a fag you talk like a fag" a remark
coming from him so absurd because so inflammable and
me 170 pounds to his 130 or 120 for God's sake so I
thought secretly "No you can't fight this man he will
only scream and yell and call cops and let you hit him

again and haunt all your dreams, there is no way to put a subterranean down on the floor or for that matter put em down at all, they are the most unputdownable in this world and new culture")—finally Wallenstein going to the head for a leak and Yuri says to me, Mardou being at the bar gathering three more wines, "Come on let's go in the john and bust him up," and I get up to go with Yuri but not to bust up Ross rather to stop anything might happen there—Yuri having been in his own in fact realer way than mine almost a hoodlum, imprisoned in Soledad for defending himself in some vicious fight in reform school —Mardou stopping us both as we head to the head, saying, "My God if I hadn't stopped you" (laughing embarrassed little Mardou smile and shniffle) "you'd actually have gone in there"—a former love of Ross's and now the bottomless toilet of Ross's position in her affections I think probably equal to mine now, O damblast the thorny flaps of the pap time page—

Going thence to the Mask as usual, beers, get worse drunk, then out to walk home, Yuri having just arrived from Oregon having no place to sleep is asking if it's allright to sleep at our place, I let Mardou speak for her own house, tho feebly say some "okay" in the middle of the confusion, and Yuri comes heading homeward with us—enroute finds a pushcart, says "Get in, I'll be a taxi-cab and push you both home up the hill."—Okay we get in, and lie on our backs drunk as only you can get drunk on red wine, and he pushes us from the Beach at that

fateful park (where we'd sat that first sad Sunday afternoon of my dream and premonitions) and we ride along
in the pushcart of eternity, Angel Yuri pushing it, I can
only see stars and occasional rooftops of blocks—no
thought in any mind (except briefly in mine, possibly
in others) of the sin, the loss entailed for the poor
Italian beggar losing his cart there—on down Broadway
clear to Mardou's, in the pushcart, at one point I push and
they ride, Mardou and I singing bop and also bop to
the tune *Are the Stars out Tonight* and just drunk—
parking it foolishly in front of Adam's and rushing up,
making noise.—Next day, after sleeping on floor with
Yuri snoring on the couch, waiting up for Adam as if
beaming to hear told about our exploit, Adam comes
home blackfaced mad from work and says "Really you
have no idea the pain you're causin' some poor old
Armenian peddler you never think that—but jeopardizing
my pad with that thing in front, supposing the cops find
it, and what's the matter with you." And Carmody saying
to me "Leo I think you perpetrated this masterpiece" or
"You masterminded this brilliant move" or such which
I really didn't—and all day we've been cutting up and
down stairs looking at pushcart which far from being cop-
discovered still sits there but with Adam's landlord
teetering in front of it, waiting to see who's going to
claim it, sensing something fishy, and of all things
Mardou's poor purse still in it where drunkenly we'd
left it and the landlord finally confiscating IT and wait-

ing for further development (she lost a few dollars and her only purse).—"Only thing that can happen, Adam, is the cops'll find the pushcart, they can very well see the purse, the address, and take it to Mardou's but all she has to say is 'O I found my purse,' and that's that, and nothing'll happen." But Adam cries, "O you even if nothing'll happen you screw up the security of my pad, come in making noise, leave a licensed vehicle out front, and tell me nothing'll happen."—And I had sensed he'd be mad and am prepared and say, "To hell with that, you can give hell to these but you won't give hell to me, I won't take it from you—that was just a drunken prank," I add, and Adam says, "This is my house and I can get mad when it's—" so I up and throw his keys (the keys he'd had made for me to walk in and out any time) at him but they're entwined with the chain of my mother's keys and for a moment we fumble seriously at the mixed keys on the floor disengaging them and he gets his and I say "No that, that's mine, there," and he puts it in his pocket and there we are.—I want to rush up and leave, like at Larry's.—Mardou is there seeing me flip again—far from helping her from flips. (Once she'd asked me "If I ever flip what will you do, will you help me?—Supposing I think you're trying to harm me?"—"Honey," I said, "I'll try in fact I'll reassure you I'm not harming you and you'd come to your senses, I'll protect you," the confidence of the old man—but in reality himself flipping more often.)—I feel great waves of dark hostility, I mean hate, malice, destructiveness flowing out of Adam in his corner chair, I can hardly sit under the withering telepathic blast and there's all that *yage* of Carmody's around the pad, in suitcases, it's too much—(it's a comedy tho, we agree it will be a comedy later)—we talk of other things—Adam suddenly flips the key back at me, it lands in my thighs, and instead of dangling it in my finger (as if considering, as if a wily Canuck calculating advantages) I boy-like jump up and throw the key back in my pocket with a little giggle, to make Adam feel better, also to impress Mardou with my "fairness"—but she never noticed, was watching something else—so now that peace is restored I say "And in any case it was Yuri's fault it isn't at all as Frank says my unqualified masterminding"—(this push-cart, this darkness, the same as when Adam in the prophetic dream descended the wood steps to see the "Russian Patriarch", there were pushcarts there)—So in the letter that I write to Mardou answering her beauty which I have paraphrased, I make stupid angry but "pretending to be fair," "to be calm, deep, poetic" statements, like, "Yes, I got mad and threw Adam's keys back at him, because 'friendship, admiration, poetry sleep in the respectful mystery' and the invisible world is too beatific to have to be dragged before the court of social realities," or some such twaddle that Mardou must have glanced at with one eye—the letter, which was supposed to match the warmth of hers, her cuddly-in-October masterpiece, beginning with the inane-if-at-all confession: "The last time I wrote a love note it turned out to be boloney" (referring to an earlier in the year half-romance with Arlene Wohlstetter) "and I am glad you are honest," or "have honest eyes," the next sentence said—the letter intended to arrive Saturday morning to make her feel my warm presence while I was out taking my hard-working and deserving mother to her bi-six-monthlial show and shopping on Market Street (old Canuck work-ingwoman completely ignorant of arrangement of mingled streets of San Francisco) but arriving long after I saw her and read while I was there, and dull—this not a literary complaint, but something that must have pained Mardou, the lack of reciprocity and the stupidity regarding my attack at Adam—"Man, you had no right to yell at him, really, it's his pad, his right"—but the letter a big defense of this "right to yell at Adam" and not at all re-sponse to her love notes—

The pushcart incident not important in itself, but what I saw, what my quick eye and hungry paranoia ate—a gesture of Mardou's that made my heart sink even as I doubted maybe I wasn't seeing, interpreting right, as so oft I do.—We'd come in and run upstairs and jumped on the big double bed waking Adam up and yelling and tousling and Carmody too sitting on the edge as if to say "Now children now children," just a lot of drunken lushes —at one time in the play back and forth between the rooms Mardou and Yuri ended on the couch together in front, where I think all three of us had flopped—but

I ran to the bedroom for further business, talking, coming back I saw Yuri who knew I was coming flop off the couch onto the floor and as he did so Mardou (who probably didn't know I was coming) shot out her hand at him as if to say OH YOU RASCAL as if almost he'd before rolling off the couch goosed her or done something playful—I saw for the first time their youthful playfulness which I in my scowlingness and writer-ness had not participated in and my old man-ness about which I kept telling myself "You're old you old sonofabitch you're lucky to have such a young sweet thing" (while nevertheless at the same time plotting, as I'd been doing for about three weeks now, to get rid of Mardou, without her being hurt, even if possible "without her noticing" so as to get back to more comfortable modes of life, like say, stay at home all week and write and work on the three novels to make a lot of money and come in to town only for good times if not to see Mardou then any other chick will do, this was my three week thought and really the energy behind or the surface one behind the creation of the Jealousy Phantasy in the Gray Guilt dream of the World Around Our Bed)—now I saw Mardou pushing Yuri with a O H Y O U and I shuddered to think something maybe was going on behind my back—felt warned too by the quick and immediate manner Yuri heard me coming and rolled off but as if guiltily as I say after some kind of goose or feel up some illegal touch of Mardou which made her purse

little love loff lips at him and push at him and like
kids.—Mardou was just like a kid I remember the first
night I met her when Julien, rolling joints on the floor, she
behind him hunched, I'd explained to them why that
week I wasn't drinking at all (true at the time, and due
to events on the ship in New York, scaring me, saying to
myself "If you keep on drinking like that you'll die you
can't even hold a simple job any more," so returning to
Frisco and not drinking at all and everybody exclaiming
"O you look wonderful"), telling that first night almost
heads together with Mardou and Julien, they so kidlike in
their naive WHY when I told them I wasn't drinking any
more, so kidlike listening to my explanation about the
one can of beer leading to the second, the sudden gut
explosions and glitters, the third can, the fourth, "And
then I go off and drink for days and I'm gone man, like,
I'm afraid I'm an alcoholic" and they kidlike and other-
generationey making no comment, but awed, curious—
in the same rapport with young Yuri here (her age)
pushing at him, Oh You, which in drunkenness I paid not
too much attention to, and we slept, Mardou and I on
the floor, Yuri on the couch (so kidlike, indulgent, funny
of him, all that)—this first exposure of the realization of
the mysteries of the guilt jealousy dream leading, from
the pushcart time, to the night we went to Bromberg's,
most awful of all.

Beginning as usual in the Mask.

Nights that begin so glitter clear with hope, let's

go see our friends, things, phones ring, people come and go, coats, hats, statements, bright reports, metropolitan excitements, a round of beers, another round of beers, the talk gets more beautiful, more excited, flushed, another round, the midnight hour, later, the flushed happy faces are now wild and soon there's the swaying buddy da day oobab bab smash smoke drunken latenight goof leading finally to the bartender, like a seer in Eliot, TIME TO CLOSE UP—in this manner more or less arriving at the Mask where a kid called Harold Sand came in, a chance acquaintance of Mardou's from a year ago, a young novelist looking like Leslie Howard who'd just had a manuscript accepted and so acquired a strange grace in my eyes I wanted to devour—interested in him for same reasons as Lavalina, literary avidity, envy—as usual paying less attention therefore to Mardou (at table) than Yuri whose continual presence with us now did not raise my suspicions, whose complaints "I don't have a place to stay—do you realize Percepied what it is not to even have a place to write? I have not girls; nothing, Carmody and Moorad won't let me stay up there any more, they're a couple of old sisters," not sinking in, and already the only comment I'd made to Mardou about Yuri had been, after his leaving, "He's just like that Mexican stud comes up here and grabs up your last cigarettes," both of us laughing because whenever she was at her lowest financial ebb, bang, somebody who needed a "mooch" was there—not that I would call Yuri a mooch in the least (I'll tread lightly on him on this point, for obvious reasons).—(Yuri and I'd had a long talk that week in a bar, over port wines, he claimed everything was poetry, I tried to make the common old distinction between verse and prose, he said, "Lissen Percepied do you believe in freedom?—then say what you want, it's poetry, poetry, all of it is poetry, great prose is poetry, great verse is poetry."—"Yes" I said "but verse is verse and prose is prose."—"No no" he yelled "it's all poetry."— "Okay," I said, "I believe in you believing in freedom and maybe you're right, have another wine." And he read me his "best line" which was something to do with "seldom nocturne" that I said sounded like small magazine poetry and wasn't his best—as already I'd seen some much better poetry by him concerning his tough boyhood, about cats, mothers in gutters, Jesus striding in the ashcan, appearing incarnate shining on the blowers of slum tenements or that is making great steps across the light—the sum of it something he could do, and did, well—"No, seldom nocturne isn't your meat" but he claimed it was great, "I would say rather it was great if you'd written it suddenly on the spur of the moment."— "But I did—right out of my mind it flowed and I threw it down, it sounds like it's been planned but it wasn't, it was bang! just like you say, spontaneous vision!"— Which I now doubt tho his saying "seldom nocturne" came to him spontaneously made me suddenly respect it more, some falsehood hiding beneath our wine yells in

[114]

a saloon on Kearney.) Yuri hanging out with Mardou and me every night almost—like a shadow—and knowing Sand himself from before, so he, Sand, walking into the Mask, flushed successful young author but "ironic" looking and with a big parkingticket sticking out of his coat lapel, was set upon by the three of us with avidity, made to sit at our table—made to talk.—Around the corner from Mask to 13 Pater thence the lot of us going, and en route (reminiscent now more strongly and now with hints of pain of the pushcart night and Mardou's OH YOU) Yuri and Mardou start racing, pushing, shoving, wrestling on the sidewalk and finally she lofts a big empty cardboard box and throws it at him and he throws it back, they're like kids again—I walk on ahead in serious tone conversation with Sand tho—he too has eyes for Mardou— somehow I'm not able (at least haven't tried) to communicate to him that she is my love and I would prefer if he didn't have eyes for her so obviously, just as Jimmy Lowell, a colored seaman who'd suddenly phoned in the midst of an Adam party, and came, with a Scandinavian shipmate, looking at Mardou and me wondering, asking me "Do you make it with her sex?" and I saying yes and the night after the Red Drum session where Art Blakey was whaling like mad and Thelonious Monk sweating leading the generation with his elbow chords, eyeing the band madly to lead them on, *the monk and saint of bop* I kept telling Yuri, smooth sharp hep Jimmy Lowell leans to me and says "I would like to make it with your chick," (like in the old days Leroy and I always swapping so I'm not shocked), "would it be okay if I asked her?" and I saying "She's not that kind of girl, I'm sure she believes in one at a time, if you ask her that's what she'll tell you man" (at that time still feeling no pain or jealousy, this incidentally the night before the Jealousy Dream)—not able to communicate to Lowell that's—that I wanted her—to stay—to be stammer stammer be mine—not being able to come right out and say, "Lissen this is my girl, what are you talking about, if you want to try to make her you'll have to tangle with me, you understand that pops as well as I do."—In that way with a stud, in another way with polite dignified Sand a very interesting young fellow, like, "Sand, Mardou is my girl and I would prefer, etc."—but he has eyes for her and the reason he stays with us and goes around the corner to 13 Pater, but it's Yuri starts wrestling with her and goofing in the streets—so when we leave 13 Pater later on (a dike bar slummish now and nothing to it, where a year ago there were angels in red shirts straight out of Genet and Djuna Barnes) I get in the front seat of Sand's old car, he's going at least to drive us home, I sit next to him at the clutch in front for purposes of talking better and in drunkenness again avoiding Mardou's womanness, leaving room for her to sit beside me at front window—instead of which, no sooner plops her ass behind me, jumps over seat and dives into backseat with Yuri who is alone back there, to wrestle again and goof

with him and now with such intensity I'm afraid to look
back and see with my own eyes what's happening and
now the dream (the dream I announced to everyone and
made big issues of and told even Yuri about) is coming
true.

We pull up at Mardou's door at Heavenly Lane and
drunkly now she says (Sand and I having decided
drunkenly to drive down to Los Altos the lot of us and
crash in on old Austin Bromberg and have big further
parties) "If you're going down to Bromberg's in Los
Altos you two go out, Yuri and I'll stay here"—my heart
sank deep—it sank so I gloated to hear it for the first
time and the confirmation of it crowned me and blessed
me.

And I thought, "Well boy here's your chance to get
rid of her" (which I'd plotted for three weeks now) but
the sound of this in my own ears sounded awfully false,
I didn't believe it, myself, any more.

But on the sidewalk going in flushed Yuri takes my arm
as Mardou and Sand go on ahead up the fish head stairs,
"Lissen, Leo I don't want to make Mardou at all, she's all
over me, I want you to know that I don't want to make
her, all I want to do if you're going out there is go to
sleep in your bed because I have an appointment tomorrow."—But now I myself feel reluctant to stay in
Heavenly Lane for the night because Yuri will be there,
in fact now is already on the bed tacitly as if, one would
have to say, "Get off the bed so we can get in, go to that

[117]

uncomfortable chair for the night."—So this more than
anything else (in my tiredness and growing wisdom and
patience) makes me agree with Sand (also reluctant)
that we might as well drive down to Los Altos and wake
up good old Bromberg, and I turn to Mardou with eyes
saying or suggesting, "You can stay with Yuri you bitch"
but she's already got her little traveling basket or weekend bag and is putting my toothbrush hairbrush and her
things in and the idea is we three drive out—which we
do, leaving Yuri in the bed.—En route, at near Bayshore in
the great highway roadlamp night, which is now nothing
but a bleakness for me and the prospect of the "weekend"
at Bromberg's a horror of shame, I can't stand it any more
and look at Mardou as soon as Sand gets out to buy ham-
burgs in the diner, "You jumped in the backseat with
Yuri why'd you do that? and why'd you say you wanted
to stay with him?"—"It was silly of me, I was just high
baby." But I don't darkly any more now want to believe
her—art is short, life is long—now I've got in full dragon
bloom the monster of jealousy as green as in any cliche
cartoon rising in my being, "You and Yuri play together
all the time, it's just like the dream I told you about
that's what's horrible—O I'll never believe in dreams come
true again."—"But baby it isn't anything like that" but
don't believe her—I can tell by looking at her she's got
eyes for the youth—you can't fool an old hand who at the
age of sixteen before even the juice was wiped off his
heart by the Great Imperial World Wiper with Sadcloth

Jack Kerouac

fell in love with an impossible flirt and cheater, this is a boast—I feel so sick I can't stand it, curl up in the back seat, alone—they drive on, and Sand having anticipated a gay talkative weekend now finds himself with a couple of grim lover worriers, hears in fact the fragment "But I didn't mean you to think that baby" so obviously hearkening to his mind the Yuri incident—finds himself with this pair of bores and has to drive all the way down to Los Altos, and so with the same grit that made him write the half million words of his novel bends to it and pushes the car through the Peninsula night and on into the dawn.

Arriving at Bromberg's house in Los Altos at gray dawn, parking, and ringing the doorbell the three of us sheepishly I most sheepish of all—and Bromberg comes right down, at once, with great roars of approval cries "Leo I didn't know you knew each other" (meaning Sand, whom Bromberg admired very much) and in we go to rum and coffee in the crazy famous Bromberg kitchen.— You might say, Bromberg the most amazing guy in the world with small dark curly hair like the hip girl Roxanne making little garter snakes over his brow and his great really angelic eyes shining, rolling, a big burbling baby, a great genius of talk really, wrote research and essays and has (and is famous for) the greatest possible private library in the world, right there in that house, library due to his erudition and this no reflection also on his big income—the house inherited from father— was also the sudden new bosom friend of Carmody and

[119]

about to go to Peru with him, they'd go dig Indian boys and talk about it and discuss art and visit literaries and things of that nature, all matters so much had been dinning in Mardou's ear (queer, cultured matters) in her love affair with me that by now she was quite tired of cultured tones and fancy explicity, emphatic daintiness of expression, of which roll-eyed ecstatic almost spastic big Bromberg almost the pastmaster, "O my dear it's such a charming thing and I think much MUCH better than the Gascoyne translation tho I do believe—" and Sand imitating him to a T, from some recent great meeting and mutual admiration—so the two of them there in the once-to-me adventurous gray dawn of the Metropolitan Great-Rome Frisco talking of literary and musical and artistic matters, the kitchen littered, Bromberg rushing up (in pajamas) to fetch three-inch thick French editions of Genet or old editions of Chaucer or whatever he and Sand'd come to, Mardou darklashed and still thinking of Yuri (as I'm thinking to myself) sitting at the corner of the kitchen table, with her getting-cold rum and coffee—O I on a stool, hurt, broken, injured, about to get worse, drinking cup after cup and loading up on the great heavy brew—the birds beginning to sing finally at about eight and Bromberg's great voice, one of the mightiest you can hear, making the walls of the kitchen throw back great shudders of deep ecstatic sound— turning on the phonograph, an expensive well-furnished completely appointed house, with French wine, refrigerators, three-speed ma-

chines with speakers, cellar, etc.—I want to look at
Mardou I don't know with what expression—I am afraid
in fact to look only to find there the supplication in her
eyes saying "Don't worry baby, I told you, I confessed to
you I was silly, I'm sorry sorry sorry—" that "I'm-sorry"
look hurting me the most as I glance side eyes to see
it. . . .

It won't do when the very bluebirds are bleak, which
I mention to Bromberg, he asking, "Whatsamatter with
you this morning Leo?" (with burbling peek under eyebrows to see me better and make me laugh).—"Nothing,
Austin, just that when I look out the window this morning the birds are bleak."—(And earlier when Mardou
went upstairs to toilet I did mention, bearded, gaunt,
foolish drunkard, to these erudite gentlemen, something
about "inconstancy," which must have surprised them
tho)—O inconstancy!

So they try anyway to make the best of it in spite of my
palpable unhappy brooding all over the place, while
listening to Verdi and Puccini opera recordings in the
great upstairs library (four walls from rug to ceiling with
things like *The Explanation of the Apocalypse* in three
volumes, the complete works and poems of Chris Smart,
the complete this and that, the apology of so-and-so
written obscurely to you-know-who in 1839, in 1638—). I
jump at the chance to say, "I'm going to sleep," it's now
eleven, I have a right to be tired, been sitting on the
floor and Mardou with dame-like majesty all this time

in the easy chair in the corner of the library (where once
I'd seen the famous one-armed Nick Spain sit when
Bromberg on a happier early time in the year played for
us the original recording of *The Rake's Progress*) and
looking so, herself, tragic, lost—hurt so much by my
hurt—by my sorriness from her sorriness borrowing—I
think sensitive—that at one point in a burst of forgiveness, need, I run and sit at her feet and lean head on
her knee in front of the others who by now don't care
any more, that is Sand does not care about these things
now, deeply engrossed in the music, the books, the brilliant conversation (the likes of which cannot be sur-
passed anywhere in the world, incidentally, and this
too, tho now tiredly. crosses by my epic-wanting brain
and I see the scheme of all my life, all acquaintances,
loves, worries, travels rising again in a big symphonic
mass but now I'm beginning not to care so much any
more because of this 105 pounds of woman and brown
at that whose little toenails, red in the thonged sandals,
make my throat gulp)—"O dear Leo, you DO seem to
be bored."—"Not bored! how could I be bored here!"
—I wish I had some sympathetic way to tell Bromberg,
"Every time I come here there's something wrong with
me, it must seem like some awful comment on your house
and hospitality and it isn't at all, can't you understand
that this morning my heart is broken and out the window
is bleak" (and how explain to him the other time I was
a guest at his place, again uninvited but breaking in at

drug smugglers placed a price on their heads.

62. A 5 peseta coin.
63. Heath Dog Violet. A low perennial plant with heart-shaped flowers found on heaths, open woods and fenland.
64. A Whippet.
65. Mastiff.
66. 4.
67. A cure for dog bites.
68. The gatherers ears were stopped, and a dog was tied to the plant's stem, pulling up the whole plant and root.
69. Because its thorns resemble a dog's canine teeth.
70. Poisonous to dogs.
71. 29 years (and 5 months).
72. A Greyhound called Low Pressure, also known as Timmy,. fathered more than 3000 puppies during the period December 1961 to November 1969.
73. The British classification of dogs is divided into 2 divisions – sporting and non-sporting, which are further divided into 6 groups. The Sporting Division is made up of 3 groups – Hounds, Gundogs and Terriers. The American Sporting Group is 1 of 7 Groups, and consists of bird or gundogs i.e. Pointers, Retrievers, Setters and Spaniels.
74. *Did not finish*, as used in sled dog racing and greyhound racing, meaning a racer did not finish the race.
75. A left turn.
76. Travois.
77. 1969.
78. Watchdogs.
79. Greyhound.
80. Approx. 7538 BC.
81. When one dog forces another to do most of the work while saving strength and ground, but winning most of the points in the competition.
82. Boxer.
83. Dingo, Border Collie, and Australian Terrier.
84. Chespeake Bay Retriever
85. A hound called Cavall.
86. True.
87. Chips.

88. Dominican Friars.
89. 2.
90. True
91. Domestic animal.
92. 30 barks per minute
93. 1835.
94. 1901.
95. An unspayed bitch.
96. Community or state legislation requiring dogs to be on leashes or muzzled on the street, or kept at home during prescribed curfew hours.
97. a. Centenary of the National Canine Defence League (NCDL)
    b. George Stubbs
    c. 1978
98. Tattooing, silicon microchip implants & nose prints.
99. a. A Truffle dog, a dog used to hunt for and root out truffles.
    b. Subterranean fungus, highly valued in cookery, generally growing under oak trees.
    c. Pigs or dogs. Dogs are preferred, as pigs like truffles and eat them.
100. a. The Dickin Medal.
    b. People's Dispensary for Sick Animals (PDSA).
    c. 18 dogs.
101. a. Pattern of woven or printed 4-pointed star check (resembling a dog's canine tooth), in a broken twill weave.
    b. Boucle fabric resembling the coat of a poodle.
    c. A rough crepe fabric made of twisted yarns woven to imitate tree bark, and nothing to do with dogs!
102. a. Germany.
    b. German for "protection dog".
    c. Type of advanced obedience and working dog training, which includes protection work.
103. Lewd behaviour, vomiting techniques, and embarassing habits.
104. a. The lowest throw of the dice.
    b. Cheated.
    c. You had gone to ruin.

105. a. Bad Latin.
    b. Bad verse.
    c. The letter R, also known as the "growling letter".

106. a. A scrap, or a quick, confused fight.
    b. Both fighters or wrestlers hit the ground together.
    c. The literal meaning is to lie still and silent, but also slang for staying quiet and out of sight.

107. a. A bitch pack of hounds.
    b. Beagles.
    c. A male hare.

108. a. Cure for a rabid dog bite.
    b. Ancient Romans swallowed the singed dog hair as a hangover cure.
    c. Scotch whiskey (1oz), double cream (1.25oz) & honey (0.5oz). Mix well and serve with ice.

109. a. Chicken.
    b. Cornmeal spoon bread.
    c. Rolled currant dumpling or jam pudding.

110. a. A staircase which goes back and forward without a stair-well.
    b. A 2-wheeled horse-drawn driving-cart with cross seats back to back.
    c. Parhelion, or mock sun – a spot on the solar halo at which light is intensified.

Breed Answers

111. Old English Sheepdog.
112. Bergamasco.
113. Harlequin Great Dane.
114. Boston Terriers.
115. Finnish Spitz (Suomenpystykorva).
116. Dalmatian.
117. Bedlington Terrier.
118. Airedale Terrier.
119. Whippet.
120. Poodle.
121. Brittany.
122. Basset Fauves de Bretagne.
123. Hungarian Puli.
124. Chihuahua.
125. Maltese.
126. Schipperke.
127. Pekingese.
128. Saluki.
129. German Shepherd Dog.
130. Mastiff group.
131. Dandie Dinmont Terrier.
132. Miniature Pinscher.
133. Born white, and the spots develop at about 10-14 days old.
134. White. (Sometimes has biscuit or cream markings).
135. Old English Sheepdog.
136. Papillon or Continental Toy Spaniel.
137. As tightly curled as possible.on the hip. Double curl preferred.
138. Isabella (fawn).
139. Grand Bleu de Gascogne.
140. False.
141. Great Dane.
142. No. The Basenji yodels.
143. New Guinea Singing Dog.
144. Coton de Tulear.
145. Lhasa Apso.

146. Chihuahua.
147. Bullmastiff.
148. Gordon Setter.
149. Gordon Setter.
150. Havanese or Bichon Havanese.
151. Irish Wolfhound.
152. Weimaraner.
153. A small Greyhound bred by King Frederick of Prussia, at his Potsdam palace.
154. Black and Tan Terrier.
155. A miniature Beagle, being less than 10 inches in height compared to the normal 13-16 inches.
156. English Toy Spaniels.
157. Alaskan Malamute.
158. Bloodhound.
159. Pomeranian.
160. Porcelaine Hounds.
161. Canaan Dog.
162. Rottweiler.
163. Yorkshire Terrier.
164. Briard, from Brie.
165. Belgian Shepherd Dog - the Groenendael.
166. The Hairless is hairless, except for soft hair on head, toes and tail. Powderpuff covered with long soft hair over body.
167. Arabian greyhound.
168. Morocco.
169. Swiss scenthounds.
170. Tosa Inu.
171. Pug.
172. Cardigan Welsh Corgi is larger and has a long foxbrush-type tail. Pembroke is smaller and has a short tail.
173. Bouvier de Flandres.
174. Rothbury Terrier.
175. Egyptian sheepdog.
176. Affenpinscher.
177. Used to nip at the heels of cattle to control them.
178. Japanese Akita.

179. Clumber Spaniel.
180. Term used to describe the medium-sized French hounds.
181. True.
182. Welsh Terrier.
183. Finnish Spitz.
184. Dobermann and Bergamsco.
185. Australian Cattle Dogs.
186. Pug.
187. Lhasa Apso.
188. Petit Basset Griffon Vendeen.
189. True.
190. Clumber Spaniel.
191. Chesapeake Bay Retriever.
192. Irish Terrier.
193. Norwich Terrier.
194. Bloodhound.
195. Turkey.
196. Borzoi.
197. Shar-Pei.
198. Keeshond.
199. Sleeve Pekingese.
200. Landseer (Newfoundland).
201. Greyhound.
202. Toy Spaniel (King Charles and Cavalier King Charles Spaniels).
203. Greyhound and Irish Wolfhound crosses, developed in Australia in the nineteenth century to hunt kangeroo.
204. Welsh Foxhound.
205. 2- smooth-coated and wire-haired.
206. No, they are separate breeds.
207. Irish Setter.
208. No, either a Labrador Retriever (yellow), or a Golden Retrieve.
209. Australia.
210. Smooth-coated Chow Chow.

Section 2

211. Bichon Frisé.

212. True.
213. Large, flat and round, with no arch – like a snowshoe. Heavily furnished with hair. Thick strong pads.
214. Airedale Terrier.
215. Chesapeake Bay Retriever.
216. Rolling, lose-jointed, shuffling and side-wise motion. Does not raise his feet very high off the ground.
217. Almond shaped and moderately deep set.
218. False. Does not have an undercoat.
219. True. Coat lightens with age.
220. Leonberger.
221. Yorkshire Terrier.
222. Webbed feet, designed for swimming.
223. Harrier.
224. Miniature Pinschers and Affenpinschers.
225. Giant Schnauzer.
226. Catahoula Leopard Dog.
227. English Setter. Ticking or roan coat colour patterns.
228. Only when the coat surrounding the eye is white.
229. It measures a Welsh yard (from the tip of its nose to the end of the outstretched tail).
230. West Highland White Terrier.
231. The black colour can appear weathered or rusty. The colour fades in the sun, and lacks intensity.
232. Weight.
233. Irish Water Spaniel.
234. Alert, kind, indicating a high-degree of intelligence.
235. The padding, or exceptional thickness of the upper lips or flews.
236. Scottish Deerhound.
237. Keeshond.
238. Finnish Spitz.
239. Mexican Hairless.
240. No. Introduced in Britain in 1947.
241. Kerry Blue Terrier.
242. Kuvacz is larger (88-114lbs, 40-52kg) than the

Maremma (77-99lbs, 35-45kg).

243. Shar Pei.
244. Italian Spinone.
245. Unshaven ring of hair on the hindquarters of the Poodle in the continental clip.
246. Curly Coated Retriever.
247. True.
248. Black or liver (a few white hairs permissible).
249. American Staffordshire Bull Terrier.
250. Boston Terrier.
251. 4 (Irish Terrier, Glen of Imaal Terrier, Soft Coated Wheaten Terrier, and Kerry Blue Terrier).
252. False. Red and white only.
253. Labrador Retriever.
254. Black.
255. Australian Kelpie.
256. Mexican Hairless Dog.
257. Malinois.
258. White Bull Terrier.
259. Co. Wicklow, Eire.
260. True.
261. French Bulldog.
262. German Shepherd Dogs.
263. Norwegian Lundehund (Puffin Dog).
264. Dandie Dinmont and Skye Terriers.
265. Briard.
266. 45 degree angle forward & downward to the shoulder joints.
267. Chinook.
268. Papillon has large upright butterfly, prick ears, and the Phalene has drop-ears.
269. Czesky or Bohemian Terrier.
270. True.
271. Portugal.
272. Basset Hound.
273. Beauceron, or Berger de Beauce.
274. Stripping comb or hand-stripping the coat, and plucking out the dead hair. Scissors only used to trim the eyebrows, leg hair and around the feet.
275. Results in a break down or weakness in the pasterns, which

have a greater than desirable slope away from the perpendicular when viewed side on. In practical terms, reduces the dog's efficiency in running, and the amount of exercise it is capable of taking.

276. Standard Schnauzer.

277. Chesapeake Bay Retrievers.

278. A Pug raised the alarm of the approach of the Spanish enemy at Hermingny in 1572, thereby saving the life of the William I, Prince of Orange.

279. The lozenge mark on the head of the Blenheim Cavalier King Charles Spaniel. Sometimes also used to refer to cheek marking on toy dogs in general.

280. Maltese dog.

281. False. The hindfeet are larger.

282. A generic term for shepherd dog, generally used for the Pyrenean Mountain Dog.

283. Schillerstovare or Schiller Hound.

284. In young puppies.

285. Tibetan Mastiff.

286. German Shepherd Dog.

287. False. The Beardie has a double coat which is shaggy but not so long as to hide the natural lines of the body. The coat must never be trimmed.

288. A French hound, named after the Chateau de Billy in Poitou.

289. 1945.

290. Australian Cattle Dog.

291. The jabot (also called the apron, and is the long hair between the front legs..

292. True, 1650.

293. Sredni – the medium sized Lowland Sheepdog.

294. Field Spaniels of 25lbs or under. (Also shown as Springer Spaniels).

295. St Bernard breed standard.

296. The short-haired saddle area, which is darker than that of the long coat.

297. Lakeland Terrier (Stingray of Derrybach).

298. English Springer Spaniel.

299. Strong, slightly crooked front legs which allow him, when

digging to throw out the earth to each side of him, and so not block his own progress.

300. 1860.
301. Swedish Vallhund (Vasgotaspets).
302. Guard and defence dogs against the native Indians.
303. Sealyham Terrier.
304. Great Britain.
305. Black and Tan Coonhound.
306. Any mixed-breed hound that has solid tan markings.
307. Foxhound.
308. Shar-Pei.
309. Wirehaired Pointing Griffon.

Section 3

310. Australian Silky Terrier. The Silky is in the Toy Group, the others are in the Terrier Group.
311. Shiba Inu. It is a Japanese breed, the others are Chinese.
312. Saluki. It originates in the Middle East, the others are both African breeds.
313. Welsh Corgi. It has a short-medium length coat. The others come in 2 different coat-types – rough and smooth.
314. Anatolian Shepherd Dog. It is a flock guarding breed, the others are herding and shepherding breeds.
315. Harrier. It is a scent hound, the others are sight hounds.
316. Rottweiler. It is a shortcoated breed, the others are long-haired, with stand-off coat.
317. Tibetan Mastiff. The others have blue-black tongues.
318. Basset Hound. It has a sabre-tail, the others have curled tails set on high.
319. Whippet. It has rose ears, the others have prick or erect ears.
320. Dandie Dinmont Terrier. It has a long, low body, the others have cobby, compact bodies.
321. Irish Water Spaniel. It is an Irish water dog, the others are English land gundogs.
322. Norwich Terrier. It is a short-legged terrier, the others are long-legged terriers.
323. Groenendael. It has a black coat, the others are born with black/dark coats which lighten as the dog matures.

324. Italian Greyhound. It is a smooth-coated toy breed, the others are members of the longer coated Bichon family

Section 4

325. Basenji.
326. Bull Terrier.
327. Kerry Blue Terrier.
328. Norfolk Terrier.
329. Saluki.
330. Saluki.
331. Saluki.
332. Irish Setter and Irish Wolfhound.
333. Cocker Spaniel.
334. Irish Setter.
335. Labrador Retriever.
336. Labrador Retriever.
337. Gordon Setter.
338. Schnauzers.
339. Pointer.
340. Pyrenean Mountain Dog.
341. Boxer
342. Great Dane
343. Deerhound.
344. Scottish Terrier.
345. Boxer.
346. Bulldog and Border Terrier.
347. Border Terrier.
348. Poodle.
349. Irish Water Spaniel.
350. Smooth Fox Terrier.
351. Samoyed.
352. Miniature Dachshund.
353. Poodle.
354. Irish Red & White Setter.
355. Border Terrier.
356. Kerry Blue Terrier.
357. Golden Retriever.
358. Basenji.
359. French Bulldog.

360. Borzoi.
361. Griffon Bruxellois.
362. Cairn Terrier.
363. Whippet.
364. Airedale Terrier.
365. Golden Retriever.
366. West Highland White Terrier.
367. Bloodhound.
368. Field Spaniel.
369. Cocker Spaniel.
370. German Spitz.
371. Hungarian Vizsla.
372. Airedale Terrier.
373. Golden Retriever.
374. Cardigan Welsh Corgi.

Section 5

375. a. A ridge of hair on the back, growing in the opposite direction to the rest of the coat.
     b. Phu-Quoc Dog, or the Mha Kon Klab.
     c. Thailand.

376. a. Haldenstovare.
     b. Scent hound.
     c. Schillerstovare, Hamiltonstovare, & Smalandsstovare.

377. a. Brabancon.
     b. Pug.
     c. Griffon d'Ecurie, or stable Griffon.

378. Smooths – Petit Brabancon.
     Rough Reds – Brussels Griffons.
     Rough other colours – Belgian Griffons.

379. a. Dachshunds.
     b. Teckel.
     c. By chest circumference.

380. a.   1st premolars.
     b.   Class 1 Certificate for Breeding.
c.   3 or more missing teeth.

381. a.   Groenendael.
     b.   Laekenois.
     2c. Malinois.

382. a.   1913.
     b.   Cream.
     c.   US and Canada.

383. a.   Shetland Sheepdog.
     b.   Colloquial for farmdog, from the Gaelic "Toon"
     meaning farm.
     c.   1906.

384. The Vendeen.   Grand Griffon-Vendeen
                     Briquet Griffen Vendeen
                     Grand Basset Griffon Vendeen
                     Petit Basset Griffon Vendeen.

385. a.   Black with tan markings; ruby; and red and white.
     b.   Tri-colour.
     c.   Prince Charles.

386. a.   Norfolk has drop-ears, the Norwich has prick-ears.
     b.   1964.
     c.   1979.

387. a.   Alaskan Malamute.
     b.   Eskimo Dog.
     c.   Siberian Husky.

388. a.   Fila Brasileiro.
     b.   Dogue de Bordeaux.
     c.   Mastiff.

389. a.   Little Lion Dog, or Petit Chien Lion.

b. Lion cut, front half of body left long to resemble a lion's mane, back half and tail clipped, leaving only a plume at the end of the tail.

c. Long, soft and silky. Can be any colour.

390. a. Maltese.
b. Chihuahua.
c. Pharoah Hound.

391. a. Coursing wolves.
b. Matched for size and speed, but also matched for coat colour and markings.

392. a. Pointer.
b. Setter.
c. Starters.

393. a. After the game is shot, the dog is sent out to pick up and retrieve.
b. Works in the open, finding and holding the game, but not retrieving. Scents the air for birds and then stays still and silent "pointing" to and holding the game.
c. Works in cover and undergrowth, finding, flushing out and retrieving game.

394. a. 5 varieties.
b. Standard (Mittel) German Spitz; Small (Klein) German Spitz.
c. Keeshond.

395. a. Jack Russell/Parson Jack Russell Terrier.
b. Hunting terrier developed to drive foxes from their underground lairs.
c. The longer-legged Parson Jack Russell, standing 14in at the shoulder.

396 a. Retrieved lost nets and tackle.
b. Courier between fishing boats .
c. Guard-dog for the boat, tackle and "catch" when ashore.

Breed Answers

397. a. Boxer.
     b. Boxer.
     c. Flock St Salvator.

398. a. Irish Red and White Setter.
     b. Irish Red and White is shorter, wider and sturdier; has higher set ear; has less heavy feathering; its skull is domed without occipital protuberance as in the Irish Setter.

399. a. All colours.
     b. Red, small white marking allowed.
     c. Black or liver.

Section 6

400. Schipperke.
401. French Bulldog.
402. Yorkshire Terrier.
403. Norfolk Terrier.
404. Chihuahua.
405. Chinese Crested.
406. Bedlington Terrier.
407. Manchester Terrier.
408. Chow Chow.
409. Keeshond.
410. Collie (Rough).
411. Pug.
412. Skye Terrier.
413. St Bernard.
414. Brussels Griffon (Griffon Bruxellois).
415. Afghan Hound.
416. Sussex Spaniel.
417. Saluki.
418. Tibetan Terrier.
419. Bloodhound.
420. Pointer.
421. Maltese.
422. Greyhound.
423. Curly-coated Retriever.

Veterinary Answers

425. Free from major faults, using the relevant breed standard as a guide.
426. Characteristics or distinguishing features required by a dog, based on the requirements of the breed standard.
427. Overall appearance and bone structure of the dog.
428. Angles created by the bones at the joints, particularly at the shoulder, stifle, hock, the pasterns and the pelvic area.
429. Has the correct range of angulation for a given breed.
430. Horses.
431. A dog's upper outline from the withers or shoulder to the base of the tail, as seen in profile.
432. Approximately 320 bones.
433. The skin.
434. 13 pairs.
435. 16, 4 per foot.
436. 3 phalanges per toe.
437. Approx. 70%.
438. Femur, or thigh bone.
439. Achilles tendon.
440. 13th rib, which remains completely unattached ventrally. Allows greater lung expansion in the chest cavity.
441. Breastbone (sternum). Also used to describe the chest or thorax.
442. The knee joint.
443. 5 – large middle and 4 digital pads.
444. Stopper pad. Protective covering around the accessory bone.
445. Bones and joints.
446. 38.5 degrees centigrade (101.5F).
447. No. Higher, 39 degrees centigrade (102F).
448. 90-100 beats per minute.
449. True.
450. 20 upper teeth, 22 lower teeth.
451. 28.
452. Close family breeding, i.e. brother to sister, father to daughter, son to mother.
453. Sense of touch.

Veterinary Questions

454. A shortage of or imbalance of calcium and phosphorus.
455. Gregor Mendel.
456. Artificial insemination.
457. Father (sire).
458. Average 63 days (9 weeks). Pregnancies lasting between 55-71 days are considered normal.
459. 10.
460. A dog's shape, size, colour, sex, temperament, state of health and intelligence.
461. A feature or defect which is present a birth.
462. A male dog in which both testicles are seen to be present in the scrotum. Unspayed bitches are also sometimes called "entire".
463. Neutering.
464. Progressive Retinal Atrophy.
465. Affects the eyes, leading to blindness.
466. Hard Pad Disease. Nose and pads often become thickened, cracked and dry.
467. The ear. It is the inflamation of the external ear canal.
468. Viral disease.
469. Ticks.
470. To prevent a injured dog hurting itself, by biting, pulling at stiches, chewing or tearing at a plaster cast or bandages.
471. The inside of the thigh – the artery just under the skin.
472. Yes.
473. To prevent bacterial placque and tartar from forming at the base of the teeth and gums. If the placque and tartar are not removed, the gums can become infected, may recede, and the dog gets bad breath.
474. Proteins, carbohydrates, fats, vitamins and minerals.
475. To avoid draughts.
476. Keeping a dog's teeth and gums healthy.
477. Chicken, game or fish boñes. These may lodge in the throat, or puncture the intestines.
478. Dog's sense of smell.
479. Minor bleeding: keeping direct pressure on the wound until bleeding stops and /or applying an ice pack. Severe bleeding: applying a tourniquet.
480. True.

481. Yes
482. A malformation of the hip joint, where the socket (acetabulum) is too shallow and/or the head of the femur (the ball) is too flat and irregular in shape. The poorly formed joint is susceptible to wear and tear leading to pain, difficulty in walking and arthritis.
483. The outer coat's guard hairs on the neck and the back are raised. This is involuntary and is caused by fear and anger. Used to impress or scare off the enemy.
484. Cutting the nail too short, and cutting through the quick, which contains the blood vessels and nerves. This is painful, and the cut may bleed freely for a short time.
485. Having well developed, strong muscles, i.e. top physical condition.
486. Overdeveloped in the shoulder blades.
487. Pasterns.
488. Canine parvovirus.
489. True.
490. Increases the length of stride.
491. Sight or gaze hounds.
492. Greyhound, which can run at 40mph over short distances.
493. 20.
494. Through their pads, mouth and tongue, but not through the skin
495. Remnants of the thumb located on the forefeet. Located on the inner surface of the pasterns on the hindfeet.
496. Keep the coat clean; prevent matting of the hair, and remove any loose hair, dust or dirt; stimulate the circulation.
497. A corded coat.
498. 2 coats. Soft undercoat for warmth, with harsher, weatherproof outercoat.
499. Coat is made up of a mass of tight curls, which trap the air and protect the dog from water and the cold.
500. Airborne infection, spread from the infected mucous or airborne droplets from a coughing dog.
501. The body's shock absorbers. Located at the junction where the paw meets the foreleg.
502. The locking together of the dog and the bitch during mating, caused by the swelling of the bulbis glandis just behind the penis.

503. Part of the bitch's milk which provides the puppies with immunity from disease.

504. Flesh-coloured, light or brown nose. Usually a breed fault, but is required by some breeds, such as the Brittany or the Pharaoh Hound.

505. The leather.

506. The bridge of the nose.

507. White and blue eyes, usually associated with merle coat colour.

508. A round eye which protrudes slightly.

509. Pads which are thin and lack cushioning.

510. Toes which point inwards.

511. Specialised feet of the Arctic breeds, adapted for rough icy terrain. Oval, firm and compact, with well-knitted, well-arched toes, and deeply cushioned pads. Webbed between the toes and well furred.

512. True.

513. Alaskan Malamute and Siberian Husky.

514. a. Rickets, poor teeth, poor muscle tone, failure to assimilate calcium and phosphorous.

b. Failure to grow, anaemia, liver disorder.

c. Rickets, bone malformations, hyper-irritability of nerves and muscles.

515. The Loin, from the end of the ribcage to the start of the pelvis.

Rules Answers

Section 1

516. 7.
517. A dog born in the US, as a result of a mating which also occurred in the US.
518. 6 months from the date of whelping. Late registration (6-12 months) will be considered if full information provided and penalty fee paid.
519. No individual puppies can be registered unless the litter was first registered by the owner or leasee of the dam at the time of whelping.
520. No litters to be registered from a dam that is less than 8 months old or over 12 years old, at the time of mating.
521. No litters to be registered sired by a dog under 7 months or over 12 years old, at the time of mating.
522. No.
523. 5 years (renewable for further 5 years).
524. Making continuous use of the kennel name. If not continuously used for a period of more than 6 years, the AKC will regard the kennel name has having been abandoned.
525. No.
526. Whether there is sufficient national interest in the new breed, and whether there is a sufficient gene pool in both numbers and diversity – usually 300-400 dogs nationally.
527. No. The AKC will only consider applications from clubs and societies, who are required to have maintained suitable and accurate pedigree/breeding records for the several generations of US-born dogs which have bred true.
528. No. Litters born outside of the US must be registered with the appropriate national kennel club.
529. An interim stage prior to a breed being eligible to compete in a variety group at AKC shows. When a new breed is eligible for registration, the breed will be placed in the Miscellaneous Class for a specified time while deciding which variety group it will join.

Rules Answers

530. Normally varies from 1-3 years before moving into a specific Variety Group.

531. Obedience and tracking events, matches, and miscellaneous classes.

532. At least 5 years after the dog has died.

533. Colour and markings.

534. AKC Investigations and Inspections Department.

535. Deals with foreign and limited registrations. Coonhound registrations are handled by the AKC/ACHA Coonhound Department which deals with registrations, pedigrees, hunt and bench show dates and results, and championship titles.

536. Show at which Championship points may be awarded, given by a club or association which is a member of the AKC.

537. A show at which championship points may be awarded, given by a club or association which is not a member of the AKC, but has obtained an AKC license to hold a specific show.

538. A show restricted to the breeds and varieties in any one group, at which championship points may be awarded.

539. A show given by a single breed club or association, at which championship points may be awarded.

540. A show restricted to American-bred dogs held by a single breed club or association, at which championship points may be awarded.

541. Informal meeting at which pure-bred dogs may compete, but no championship points are awarded. Meeting may be held by variety of clubs, but need the sanction of the AKC.

542. Member clubs and associations can hold 1 show and 1 field trial without payment of a fee to the AKC. Any additional fees or trials can be held upon payment of a fee to the AKC. Non-member clubs and associations must apply to the AKC for permission to hold specific shows, and pay the relevant fee.

543. When the Member club or association fails to hold a show at least once in 2 consecutive years. The AKC then has the right to grant another club or association permission to hold a show within the limits of the show territory of the original club or association.

544. 6 months, except at sanctioned matches when approved by the AKC.
545. Champions.
546. Class for dogs 6 months or over, born in the US, Canada, Mexico or Bermuda, which have not, prior to the date of closing of entries, won 3 First Prizes in the novice class, a 1st prize in Bred-by-Exhibitor, American-bred, or Open classes, nor one or more points towards their Championships.
547. Class for any dog 6 months or over, except in a Member Speciality Club Show held only for American-bred dogs, in which case Open Classes will be for American-bred dogs only.
548. Class divided by sex, each division only open to undefeated dogs of the same sex which have won 1st prizes in either Puppy, Twelve-to-Eighteen Month, Novice, Bred-by-Exhibitor, American-Bred, or open Classes. After Winners Prize awarded, the 2nd prize winning dogs, if undefeated except by the dog awarded Winners, shall compete with other eligible dogs for Reserve Winners. No eligible dog may be withheld from competition. Winners Class shall be allowed at shows where American-Bred and Open Classes shall be given. Winners receive the points at the show.
549. No.
550. Best of Breed, or Best of Variety.
551. 15 points, which entitles the dog to have "Ch." used before its name.
552. A dog can earn from 1 – 5 points at a show.
553. Points are awarded on the number of dogs in the actual competition, with more points being awarded for larger classes. AKC compile an annual schedule which will determine the number of points required for different breeds, sex, and geographical location.
554. The 15 points must be won under at least 3 different judges, and must include 2 "majors" (wins of 3-5 points) won under 2 different judges.
555. To obtain an Obedience title. A "leg" being an obedience test score of at least 170 out of a maximum 200 points, and a score of more than 50% on each exercise.

556. Novice, Open, and Utility.
557. Tests, held under AKC regulations, which require a dog to follow a trail by scent.
558. TDX stands for Tracking Dog Excellent, an award given for success in the advanced tests.
559. Yes.
560. Title given to a dog that has successfully completed the highest level of the 3 Hunting Tests.
561. Testing and Trial sections.
562. An award given to a dog which shows an inherent herding ability and is trainable in herding.
563. An award given to a dog which has basic herding training, and can herd a small group of livestock through a simple course.
564. 15 Championship points.

Section 2

565. Full and Associate members.
566. a. Full.
     b. Full.
     c. Full.
     d. Full.
     e. Associate.
     f. Associate.
     g. Full.
     h. Full.

567. Each full member sends 3 delegates who together have only 1 vote.
568. 4 years, but can be re-elected.
569. Twice a year.
570. Europe, America, Asia, Africa, Oceania and Australia.
571. President, Vice-President, and Treasurer.
572. Legal, Scientific, and Standards Commissions.
573. English, French, German and Spanish.
574. A list of their national breeds, and corresponding breed standards, which must be set out according to the model adopted by the FCI.

575. The General Assembly. Modifications and new provisional standards are approved by the General Committee
576. The Standards Commission, and if a new breed is to be admitted the advice of the Scientific Commission must be sought.
577. Simultaneously in the 4 official languages.
578. Yes.
579. Yes, but those granted by its affiliated organisations.
580. Yes.
581. All-Breeds and International Trials at which the FCI awards international championship certificates.
582. The governing national bodies retain responsibility for their own judges, but they must be recognized by the FCI.
583. A list of recognised judges with a list of the breeds or groups which they are entitled to judge.
584. 10 Groups.
585. Championship Aptitude Certificate of International Beauty.
586. International Dog-Show with attribution of the FCI CACIB.
587. Minimum of 4, with an extra one granted for every additional 5,000 dogs registered in the national Stud Book.
588. Only 1 can be awarded on the same day and at the same place.
589. Open, working and Champion Classes.
590. Title of International Champion of Beauty of the FCI, or a title of National Champion in a country affiliated to the FCI.
591. 15 months.
592. A dog drawing very close to the ideal breed standard, and which is in perfect condition. It should also have the characteristics of its sex.
593. A dog which is sufficiently typed without notable qualities, or not in very good physical condition.
594. Open, working or Championship Classes, to the exclusion of other classes.
595. No.
596. Yes, if invited.
597. 4 CACIBS in 3 different countries, given by 3 different judges, whatever the number of competitors. One CACIB must be obtained in the owner's country of residence, or the country of origin of the breed.
598. 25 years old.

Rules Answers

599. Breed knowledge, and ring procedure.
600. Breed, Group and All Round Judge.
601. Up to 80 dogs per day.
602. Up to 150 dogs per day.
603. Agility European Championships.
604. Maximum of 8 dogs.
605. Personal record of a dog's competition scores, which is compulsory for FCI competitions.
606. Field Trials.
607. Decision that CACIT should be awarded solely at trials organized on live game, and the trials should have the character of practical hunting, organized on natural game.
608. Field Trials for Retriever Breed Dogs.
609. Partridge.
610. Minimum of 2 and maximum of 4.
611. Odedience and defence, and tracking.
612. 3. International Competition Classes 1-3.
613. Mediocre.

Section 3

614. Championship Show, Open Show and Open Parade.
615. Yes.
616. Exhibition of registered dogs, at which Champion dogs may not compete, and at which no Challenge Certificate points are awarded. Regarded as the training ground for new exhibitors.
617. Championship Show.
618. Informal gathering by a non-affiliated club or society, which has asked permission from canine governing authority to hold a sanctioned event.
619. For dogs of 3 months and under 6 months of age.
620. For dogs over 18 and not over 36 months of age.
621. For dogs 6 months of age or over which have not won a 1st prize at any Open Parade or Championship Show.
622. For dogs 6 months or older whelped in the State in which it is exhibited.
623. For dogs 6 months or older whelped in Australia.
624. For all dogs of 6 months or over. May be confined to

specific breed or variety at Championship or Breed Shows.

625. 7.
626. 4.
627. A dog can only have the highest Obedience title after its name.
628. No Novice only for dogs of any breed, 6 months or over, which are not eligible for the title of Companion Dog (CD).
629. Companion Dog Excellent, a certificate obtained through receiving 3 scores of 170 points or more in Utility Classes.
630. Minimum 3 and maxiumum of 10.
631. No, unless specifically requested, dogs are generally given the opportunity to complete the Trial exercises.
632. Utility Dog Class.
633. Minimum length must be 750mm.
634. "Heel on lead", and "Stand for Examination".
635. Enters and leaves on the lead.
636. 3 different varieties.
637. If the handler continuously tugs at the lead.
     If the handler adapts his pace to the dog.
     If the dog does not complete the principle feature of the exercise.
638. 200 points
639. A dog must have a Companion Dog (CD) title, and have passed the Preliminary Tracking qualification title.
640. Must successfully complete Test 1 & 2, tracking 1 known person and one unknown person.
641. A person (known to the handler or unknown depending on the test) who places articles on the track at places nominated by the judge, and places an additional article at the start of each track. The tracklayer follows the track marked out earlier collecting all the flags along the way. At the end of each track, he remains silent and still, waiting to be found.
642. 18 months of age.
643. 4 dogs, and 4 different owners.
644. 3, with a least 2 different judges.
645. Finishing in the top half of the number of dogs competing in the 2nd round of a trial, or having completed a faultless round in either the 1st or 2nd round at the same trial. Only 1

qualifiying card gained at a Specialist Breed Agility Trial will be accepted.

646. 450mm.

647. Maxmimum number of 30.

648. No.

649. A bonus 5 second deduction from the final time for a specific round.

650. 5 seconds added to the course time for each mistake or fault.

651. "Are you ready"?

652. Penalty for misbehaviour.

653. Brittany, German Shorthaired Pointer, German Wirehaired Pointer, Large Munsterlander, Hungarian Vizsla, and the Weimaraner.

654. Yes.

655. To seek and retrieve fallen game, when ordered to do so. He should sit quietly with the handler, or anywhere where the handler was directed him to, until ordered to retrieve.

656. 12 points in Non-Retrieving trials. Gained by winning outright a Championship Stake or National Championships, or by winning outright 2 All Age Stakes, or by being placed 2nd in 2 Championship Stakes or National Championships, or winning outright 1 All Age Stake and being placed 2nd in a Championship Stake or National Championships.

657. Quail.

658. Minimum of 6 runners, belonging to at least 4 different owners.

659. No.

660. Only 1.

661. A discretionary award given by the judge if a dog has shown that it is not gun-shy, and that it will hunt, point and back naturally.

662. Double rise, the 2nd object of game being thrown while the dog is returning with the first.

Section 4

663. 6 groups.

664. 3 – Hounds, Gundogs and Terriers.

665. A separate register for imported dogs of new and

unregistered breeds. May be transfered to the normal breed register, at a later date, if there is sufficient interest shown in the new breed. Also includes imported dogs, which although already recognised, have had no registrations for 10 years.

666. Any type of dog, whether pure-bred or mongrel. A restrictive form of registration, with dogs limited to only Obedience and Working Trial competitions.

667. A dog's name cannot be changed after 30 days from the date at which the dog qualified for entry in the Stud Book, ie. 30 days after it won its first qualifying award.

668. The registered owner's restrictions placed on his dog's records, which may prevent the dog from taking part in shows and other licensed competitions; prevent its offspring from being registered; prevent the dog from being exported; and prevent anyone changing the dog's name.

669. No, only registered after leaving 6 month quarantine, and only if the Kennel Club has a reciprocal agreement with national canine authority from the country of origin.

670. No, a dog must be registered before it leaves the country.

671. No. A dog with cropped ears is barred from competing in any licensed event.

672. 8 years old.

673. 6 litters.

674. Hounds bred by recognised British Hunts.

675. Change of name applied for.

676. Masters of Harriers and Beagles Association.

677. Breed, General, Dog Training, Agility and Ringcraft Societies.

678. Large agricultural or municipal societies or associations, which wish to include a licensed dog show, as part of a much larger agricultural or civic event.

679. A national list of recognised ringcraft societies.

680. A Council made up of representatives of registered breed societies, which provide specialist knowledge and advice on their breed. Can make representations to the General Committe of the Kennel Club regarding the breed standard, and on applications to register new breed societies.

681. 1 licensed show per year.

682. Annually, every Jaanuary.
683. 7.
684. Sanction, Primary, Exemption Shows, and Matches.
685. Show at which registered and unregistered dogs can compete. May be held by an unregistered society, which applied to the Kennel Club for permission to hold it.
686. Show which is restricted to members of a Show Society, providing up to 10 classes if a single breed show, or up to 25 classes if more than 1 breed to be exhibited.
687. Must not be less than 500 sq feet of floor space.
688. Minimum of 4 awards.
689. 6 months old.
690. Yes.
691. At shows featuring more than 1 breed.
692. If won in a breed class for which no Challenge Certificate was on offer.
693. 5 or more point green stars.
694. A gundog or Collie dog that has won 3 Challenge Certificates, under 3 different judges, with one Challenge Certificate being given when the dog is over 12 months of age.
695. A dog which is 7 years old or above, which can compete in the Veteran Classes.
696. 3 or more belonging to 1 exhibitor. The dogs must be individually entered into classes apart from team or brace.
697. Obedience shows.
698. Agility Tests.
699. A walk plank (4'6" high x 12-14' long, and 10-12" wide) with fixed ramps on each end. Last 3ft of each ramp painted a different colour to show where the dog must land.
700. 18 months, except Bloodhounds who can compete when 12 months old.
701. Patrol Dog (PD) and Tracking Dog (TD) Stakes.
702. No.
703. A Club or inter-Club competition, but only amongst registered clubs and societies.
704. When the dog is seen to approach and unhesitatingly pick out a runner from a group of 3 at the end of the line.
705. Only if the dog has gained both sections of the Working

Permit issued by the Association of Bloodhound Breeders or the Bloodhound Club, which certifies that they are steady with farm animals.

706. Retrievers and Irish Water Spaniels.
Sporting Spaniels other than Irish Water Spaniels.
Pointers and Setters.
Hunt, Point and Retrieve breeds.

707. A Warrant issued to a dog that has won 25 points between the ages of 12 to 18 months old. The scale of points varies but includes 3 points for first prizes in a breed class at a Championship Show where Challenge Certificates were on offer. Open show wins and other breed class wins only count as 1 point.

708. Postgraduate.

709. Up to 100 dogs.

710. 3 refusals or 3 run outs.

711. A breed standard of recognised breed which has not been granted Challenge Certificates.

712. A number allocated to a dog who has won a Challenge Certificate, Reserve Challenge Certificate, or a qualifying palce in the classes which are in the Band for their breed. Also dogs winning qualifying awards at Field Trials, Working Trials, and Champion Obedience Awards.

Show Answers

713. Newcastle-upon-Tyne, June 28 & 29 1859.
714. Pointers and Setters.
715. 60.
716. Birmingham, 1860.
717. The American Kennel & Sporting Field, by Arnold Burges, 1876.
718. No awards given.
719. Pointer and Setter Show, Mineola, New York, October 7th 1874.
720. The Kennel Club.
721. 1865, Southill.
722. 1874 Tennessee Sportsmen's Association combined dog show & field trial at Memphis.
723. May 8-10 1877.
724. Public demand to view the 1201 dogs entered.
725. Kentucky Derby.
726. Birmingham National (1860).
727. The Hound Show, Peterborough.
728. The Hound Show, Peterborough, 1879.
729. Scottish National Exhibition of Sporting and Other Dogs, February 20-22, 1871, Glasgow.
730. 1882.
731. Royal Melbourne Show.
732. Early pre-1859 dog shows, informal gatherings usually in pubs and taverns.
733. Early American dog shows, usually limited to members of clubs or societies, 1884-1895.
734. Westminster Dog Show because it is held in Madison Square Garden Centre, New York.
735. Manchester Championship Dog Show, the 2nd oldest continuously held dog show in the world.
736. Terriers.
737. 1891.
738. 1991 (Centenary show)....
739. The Kennel Club..
740. Stopped when the Kennel Club took over Crufts, which became the premier British dog show.

741. Cruft's Exhibition of Terriers, 1890.
742. Crufts 1915.
743. Crufts 1892. Alexandra, Princess of Wales's Pomeranian; Grand Duke Nicholas of Russia's Borzoi; and Prince Henry of Battenburg's Collie.
744. June 8th 1895, Ranelagh Club, Barn Elms.
745. Scottish Kennel Club's 40th Show, 1923.
746. Ladies' Kennel Association own Championship status, which was not recognised by the Kennel Club. LKA winners received silver/enamelled medals. On winning 3 medals, the dog held the title of LKA Champion, the wins were recorded in the LKA's own stud book and were published in the Ladies' Kennel Journal.
747. Paignton & District Fanciers Association's Show, 1930.
748. Belfast Championship Dog Show.
749. September 30 – October 2 1926. The Sesquicentennial, or Sesqui Show at Philadelphia, commemorating the nation's sesquicentenary, 1776-1926.
750. Westminster Kennel Club.
751. Ch Barberryhill Bootlegger, Sealyham Terrier.
752. 1928.
753. Primley Sceptre, Greyhound.
754. November 17-18, 1984. Centennial Dog Show & Obedience Trial, Philadephia Civic Centre.
755. Ch Cory Tucker Hills Manhattan, German Shepherd Dog.
756. Sh Ch Raycroft Socialite, Clumber Spaniel.
757. William L Kendrick.
758. Leonard Pagliero.
759. Crufts Centenary Show, 1991.
760. July 23-25 1988, Canberra, at "Australian Day" weekend.
761. Irish Kennel Club.
762. Charles Cruft.
763. Kennel Club's 70th Championship Show, October 7-8 1931.
764. Bala, Wales, 1873.
765. King's Kelpie.
766. Government House, and Canberra House, the official residence of the British High Commissioner.
767. Canberra dog shows.
768. French Bulldog Club of America.

769. West of England Ladies' Kennel Society.

770. Worcester, Herefordshire & Gloucestershire.

771. Foxhound and hunt terrier show, which is associated with the development of the Fox Terrier.

772. By weight. Large terriers over 9lbs, small terriers under 9lbs.

773. Manchester Terrier (Black and Tan Terriers).

774. Norwich Terrier......

775. Westminster Dog Show, 1928.

776. Midland Counties Canine Society (originally Leamington & County Canine Society).

777. National Invitational Championship Show, 1992.

778. April 1973.

779. 1975.

780. Leicester City Canine Society Ch. Show.

781. Prior to Blackpool 1939, all 2-day shows were run as 1 event, and all dogs had to return for the 2nd day. Blackpool obtained permission to hold the show as 2 separate day shows, allowing dogs to go home after the 1st day.

782. Crufts, Scottish Kennel Club and Welsh Kennel Club.

783. 1899.

784. Electricians strike at Olympia.

785. British epidemic of Foot and Mouth Disease.

786. General, group, and breed.

787. Crufts.

788. Houston, Texas.

789. 1900.

790. Newfoundland.

791. 1947.

792. 1970.

793. Championship stakes for all AKC registerable pointing breeds, who have won or been placed in AKC licensed or member club stakes, with at least 8, 13, or 17 starters. Gundog stake either open or amateur, or amateur/open or amateur/limited.

794. Her Majesty The Queen's estate at Sandringham, Norfolk.

795. Gordon Setters.

796. Speciale Venerie.

797. Classes for groups of 6, and full packs.

798. Total of 4, 2 each Spring and Autumn.
799. 5. 4 Nationals and 1 International.
800. 1932.
801. 1936 (Mount Kisco, New York).
802. Leonard Brumby, Snr. Memorial Trophy for Top Junior Handler, at Westminster Dog Show.
803. Mrs Challinor Ellis, judged Basset Hounds, at the 3rd Ladies' Kennel Association Show, 1897.
804. An individual qualified to judge a large number of breeds.
805. 1947.
806. Sweden and Australia.
807. R.A.S. Kennel Control, 1966.
808. Amsterdam All-Winners Dog Show.
809. Paris Dog Show.
810. Stockholm Dog Show.
811. New Zealand Kennel Club's Tux Show.
812. Berne, Switzerland.

Organisations Answers

Section 1

813. Federation Cynologique Internationale.
814. Royal Society for the Prevention of Cruelty To Animals.
815. Scottish Society for the Prevention of Cruelty to Animals.
816. Irish Society for the Prevention of Cruelty to Animals.
817. International Sheep Dog Society.
818. American Kennel Club.
819. British Veterinary Association.
820. Australian National Kennel Control.
821. New Zealand Kennel Club.
822. The Kennel Club.
823. Dog Writers' Association of America.
824. NCDL (National Canine Defence League).
825. German Shepherd Dog League and Club of GB founded in 1924. Originally called Alsatian League and Club of GB.
826. The Old English Sheepdog Club founded in 1888.
827. To hold Working Trials.
828. The Sheepdog Workers Association.
829. La Societe Royale Saint-Hubert.
830. Societe de Venerie.
831. Musee de la Venerie at Senlis; Musee Internationale de la Chasse at Gien.
832. Leeds Castle, Kent.
833. Birmingham Museum & Art Gallery.
834. Zoological Museum, Tring, Hertfordshire (now part of the Natural History Museum).
835. Dog Museum of America.
836. Soft-Coated Wheaten Terrier Club of America.
837. Pharaoh Club of England; Pharaoh Club of America, Inc.
838. American Bulldog.
839. United Kennel Club.
840. The Dutch Barge Dog Club (1925).
841. American Kennel Club.
842. American Dog Owners Association.
843. American Dog Owners Association.

844. Guide Dogs for the Blind Association. It breeds and trains all their own dogs.

845. Dogs' Home, Battersea.

846. The Retired Greyhound Trust.

847. Angell Memorial Hospital, Boston.

848. National Veterinary Medical Association.

849. A "Pets As Therapy" dog, which is taken by their owner into hospitals, old people's homes, etc. to spend time with patients and residents.

850. PRO-DOGS National Charity.

851. Belgium 1859. Belgian sheepdogs were used officially on night duty by the Ghent police.

852. Royal Navy.

853. Fund for the Replacement of Animals in Medical Experiments.

854. Trained to recognise certain sounds, and to alert their owners by touch when these sounds occur i.e. door bell, telephone ringing, and alarm clocks ringing.

855. National Beagle Club (US) established 1888. The Beagle Club formed later in 1890.

856. Siberian Husky Dog Club of GB.

857. Wolf Society of GB.

858. Swiss Alpine Club.

859. Royal Army Veterinary Corps.

860. New Zealand.

861. Singapore Kennel Club.

862. American Kennel Club.

863. Singapore Kennel Club.

864. Kennel Union of Southern Africa.

865. German Kennel Club (Verband fur das Deutsche Hundewesen).

866. South Africa.

867. Berne.

868. Oslo.

869. Ramat Gan.

870. Aubervillers.

871. Toronto.

872. Royal Agricultural Society Kennel Control, New South Wales.

873. North Australian Canine Association.
874. Australia.
875. Australia.
876. Irish Kennel Club.
877. Centenary of the Scottish Kennel Club.
878. Group established in 1953 to co-ordinate canine activities in Denmark, Finland, Norway & Sweden.
879. 1873.
880. 1884.
881. National Field Trial Club.
882. American Kennel Club.
883. 1888.
884. America.
885. 1884.
886. Independent kennel club, which has reciprocal agreements with other National kennel clubs, including Britain.
887. 1973.
888. 1964.
889. 1956.
890. 1911.
891. Thuin, Belgium.
892. 1874.
893. 1878.
894. 1925.
895. 1858.

Section 2

896. Univerity of Toronto School of Medicine, Canada.
897. Approx. 70%.
898. Royal Navy, Great Britain.
899. 1977.
900. The Master Eye Institute, founded in 1926.
901. To provide nation-wide protection for children and animals.
902. George T Ansell, who established the Massachusetts Society for the Protection of Animals.
903. The Tail-Waggers' Club & World League for Dog Welfare.
904. News of the World.

905. International Rescue Dog Organisation (IRO).

906. Events staged in Britain to promote working dogs in society.

907. Guide Dogs for the Blind Association. The theme summarising the partnership between guide dogs and their owners.

908. Joint Animal Committee, made up of a representatives of British animal charities, vet associations & local authorities.

909. Inter-Groom.

910. Scotsmen living abroad could be admitted to the Club.

911. An Afghan Hound not a Greyhound.

912. Confederation Canina Americana. An amalgamation of national kennel clubs in South America.

913. Gait: observing dogs in motion, 1974.

914. National Dog Club.

915. In 1736, freemasons were excommunicated by Pope Clement XII, some set up a new order to continue the old traditions, and the new organisation was named The Order of the Pug.

916. Commemorates the Pug as the royal dog of the House of Orange.

917. Pekingese.

918. The Blue Cross.

919. Frankfurt, Germany.

920. 16.

921. Association formed to sort out the confusion regarding the various Eastern breeds, i.e. Lhasa Apso, Shihi Tzu, Japanese Chins, etc.

922. Mastiffs. Prefix for Old English Mastiff Club.

923. Professional Handlers Association or Dog Handlers Guild.

924. Verein Fur Deutsch Schaferhunde (S.V.).

925. The Dachshund Club established in 1881, the Deutsch Teckelklub established in 1888.

926. Association formed in 1873 in Russia to protect and promote the older type of Borzoi.

927. Government could mobilise all privately owned Elkhounds for carrying military supplies over snow, in time of war.

928. Black East European Shepherd (developed from GSDs brought to Russia in the 1920's).

929. To promote the welfare and acceptance of the Dingo.

930. Australian Native Dog Training Society.
931. Danish Kennel Club.
932. Japanese Government. Reflected Japanese concern over the export and cross-breeding of native Japanese breeds. Declared all native breeds national monuments/treasures to provide official protection.
933. Music hall and stage animals who were forced to perform dangerous tricks, such as dogs thrown up into the air, spinning and then landing on one front leg.
934. Dogs' Home, Battersea.
935. Australian National Kennel Control.
936. Hound Trailing Association.
937. No. Only clubs and organisations can be members of the AKC.
938. Yes. Private members club, with no club or group membership.
939. Guide dogs for the blind movement.
940. 1993.
941. Annually.
942. Kennel Club of Japan.
943. 1928.
944. National Greyhound Racing Club.
945. United Kennel Club.
946. The Greyhound Hall of Fame.
947. 1912 (30 October).
948. United Kennel Club.
949. The official stud book.
950. 1905.
951. The Danish Kennel Club founded in 1897, the Norwegian Kennel Club was founded in 1898.
952. Individual membership, with individuals elected. after serving an apprentice period.
953. Ladies Kennel Association (LKA).
954. The Quaker Oats Company.

Section 3

955. a. 14th April 1949.
     b. Royal Agricultural Society's Showground, during the

Royal Easter Show.

c.   Co-ordinating and recommendary body, not an overall controlling body such as the AKC or KC. Also maintains central register of prefixes.

956. Canberra Kennel Association.
Canine Association of Western Australia.
Canine Control Council (Queensland).
Kennel Control Council (Tasmania).
Kennel Control Council (Victoria).
Northern Australian Canine Association.
RAS Kennel Control, NSW.
South Australian Canine Association.

957.   All Breed; Obedience; Tracking.

958. a.   Waterloo Cup.
b.   Annual greyhound racing event held in February at Altcar.

959. a.   Bord na gCon.
b.   Tucson, Arizona.
c.   1951.

960. a.   American Veterinary Medical Association.
b.   UK – 1844; US – 1883.
c.   Professional governing bodies maintaining national registers of veterinarians.

961. a.   London 1978.
b.   30.
c.   Aimed to provide forum for the exchange of national views leading to closer understanding. Set tradition for future meetings.

962. a.   September 1982.
b.   American Kennel Club, New York.
c.   St Louis, Missouri.

963. a.   Rooms at the Philadelphia Kennel Club.

b. 14.
c. 1929 (Pure Bred Dogs. Title changed in 1938 to The Complete Dog Book).

964. a. London.
     b. 12.
     c. 1880.

965. a. 1974.
     b. 1899.
     c. 1978.

966. a. The film was called "221" (the street number of the AKC headquarters in New York at the time).
     b. A guide to the work of the AKC. Aimed at dog clubs and societies.
     c. AKC Librarian, Beatrice Peterson Agazzi.

967. Alaskan Malamute.
     American Foxhound.
     Beagle.
     Black 'n Tan Coonhound.
     Boston Terrier.
     Chesapeake Bay Retriever.
     Cocker Spaniel (American).
     Rough Collie.

968. a. 1880.
     b. 1889.
     c. American Field (originally called The Chicago Field).

969. a. Rescue dogs used during the London Blitz to find people trapped in the bombed buildings.
     b. Locating aircraft's black box flight recorders after a plane has crashed.
     c. Search dogs always wear a harness, patrol dogs wear a collar.

970. a. 1940
     b. German Shepherd Dogs

c.   All recruits originally pet dogs given as gifts from the general public.

971. a.   Royal Society for the Protection of the Animals (RSPCA.
b   Rev. Arthur Broome.
c.   Queen Victoria.

972. a.   Dogs for the Deaf.
b.   Claims the same access rights as guide dogs for the blind.
c.   Dogs have a blaze orange collar and lead. Owner carries photo I.D..

973. a.   Assistance Dogs and People Together.
b.   Assistance Dogs for the Disabled.
c.   SOHO Foundation.

974. a.   People's Dispensary for Sick Animals.
b.   Whitechapel, in the East End of London.
c.   To provide free treatment for sick animals if owners cannot afford private veterinary fees.

975. a.   The Blue Cross.
b.   Victoria, London.
c.   The League was very active in the 1st World War, caring for the thousands of animals used by the army. The logo was adopted to distinguish it from the Red Cross when working in the battlefields.

976. a.   Irish Coursing Club.
b.   15 September - 10 March.
c.   US - American National Waterloo Cup.

977. a.   Whippet Racing Association.
b.   Whippet Coursing Club.
c.   WRA races dogs registered by the Kennel Club competing on a standardized handicapping system of yard

per pound of weight. The WCC organized coursing races during the coursing season (September-March).

978 a.   John F Kennedy International Airport, New York.
b.   Trained to sniff out prohibited produce or food, such as fresh fruit, meats, soil, plants and birds. The Beagles are not trained to sniff out drugs.
c.   Beagle sniffs passengers' luggage, and if successful the dog is trained to give a passive response by sitting down next to and pointing to the passenger or their luggage.

Personalities Answers

Section 1

979. Louis Dobermann.
980. Elizabeth Barratt Browning.
981. Rev. John Russell known as Parson Jack Russell.
982. Well-known Cumberland huntsman who ran his own pack of hounds for over 40 years. Born in 1776 and died in 1854.
983. Charles Cruft.
984. King Canute.
985. St Bernard, who founded 2 hospices for travellers in the Swiss Alps, which became famous for using dogs (St Bernards) to rescue lost travellers.
986. Sewallis E Shirley.
987. James M Taylor.
988. Richard Gibson.
989. B G Jacobs.
990. Chauncy Z. Bennett.
991. General George Patton.
992. General Douglas MacArthur.
993. George, Lord Byron.
994. Adolf Hitler.
995. Laika.
996. Belka & Strelka.
997. Sir Walter Scott.
998. Alexandra, Princess of Wales, later Queen Alexandra.
999. James Watson, author of The Dog Book, 1905.
1000. Diogenes.
1001. $15 million.
1002. Duke of Gloucester.
1003. Cavalier King Charles Spaniel.
1004. King George VI and Queen Elizabeth.
1005. The World Cup Trophy, which had been stolen.
1006. Rats.
1007. Marjorie.
1008. Duke of Gordon.

1009. Ian Dunbar.
1010. Geraldine Rockefeller Dodge.
1011. Lucy Dawson.
1012. Phil Drabble.
1013. Thomas Fall.
1014. Sir Martin Frobisher and crew on his expedition searching for the North West Passage, 1577.
1015. King Charles II.
1016. Wally Herbert.
1017. 45.
1018. German Shepherd Dogs.
1019. Eadweard Muybridge.
1020. Ivan Pavlov.
1021. Master McGrath.
1022. Helen Keller.
1023. Thelma Gray.
1024. Count A P Hamilton.
1025. Puli.
1026. Sussex Spaniels.
1027. Jimmy or Jemmy Shaw.
1028. Basenji.
1029. Madame de Pompadour.
1030. Chinese Crested Dog.
1031. General George Custer.
1032. One of General Howe's foxhounds. It has strayed across into American lines, and was identified by the inscription on its collar.
1033. August Belmont, Jnr., President of the AKC.
1034. Spent 30 years as a dog food salesman for Spratts, ending up as General Manager.
1035. August Belmont, Jnr - 27 years.
1036. Duchess of Newcastle.
1037. American Pit Bull Terriers.
1038. President Eisenhower.
1039. Shannon, a Cocker Spaniel.
1040. She was the daughter of the Russian astronaut dog Strelka.
1041. President Johnson accepted the Collie as a gift from all the children of America.
1042. Checker was a black and white Cocker Spaniel, which the

Nixon family received as a present and kept as the family pet.

1043. Laekenois – Belgian Shepherd Dog.

1044. Blenheim Spaniel, variety of King Charles and Cavalier King Charles Spaniels, named after Blenheim Palace, home of Marlborough.

1045. Commodore Matthew Perry.

1046. Pyrenean Mountain Dog (Great Pyrenees).

1047. Great Dane.

1048. Kerry Blue Terrier.

1049. Afghan Hound.

1050. Colette.

1051. Jacqueline Susan.

1052. Rhodesian Ridgebacks.

1053. Bullmastiff.

1054. Captain G A Graham.

1055. Henry VIII.

1056. Roswell Eldridge, an American who on a visit to England in 1926, offered an annual prize for King Charles Spaniels at Crufts.

1057. King Edward VII.

1058. English Setter.

1059. Fox Terrier.

1060. Lord Lonsdale.

1061. Bill Cosby.

1062. James Hinks of Birmingham.

1063. O P Smith.

1064. Napoleon Bonaparte.

1065. Scottish Terrier.

1066. The German Shepherd was originally called Kiss, and Frank found this name too embarassing.

1067. Racing Greyhound, which won the Derby 2 consecutive times, and won 46 of out his 61 races.

1068. J Lloyd Price, of Rhiwlas, Bala, who organised the first trial in 1873.

1069. Carl Spitz.

1070. George Washington.

1071. King Charles I.

1072. Geoffrey Howe.

Personalities Answers

1073. Edward VIII, Duke of Windsor.
1074. Lady Kitty Ritson, who first introduced the breed into GB.
1075. Frank Jones, Whip to the Norwich Staghounds.
1076. Cecil Aldin.
1077. Labrador Retriever.

Section 2

1078. C Steadman Hanks, of the Seacroft Kennels.
1079. Fox Terrier.
1080. Howard Knight.
1081. Lord George Scott.
1082. Earl of Malmesbury.
1083. Theodore Roosevelt.
1084. Professor Raymond Triquet.
1085. Dr Antonio Nores Martinez, who wanted a tough guard-dog, but trustworthy family dog.
1086. Czesky Terriers.
1087. American hunter, who was one of the most successful promoters of the American Blue Gascon Hound. Wrote "Big 'N' Blue" short stories about the Old Line strain, and got the breed its nickname.
1088. Mrs Wingfield-Digby.
1089. William E Buckley, President of the AKC.
1090. Sigmund Freud.
1091. Hamish MacInnes, leader of Glencoe mountain rescue team.
1092. Mr & Mrs Milton Seeley.
1093. King Henry III.
1094. Badge worn by pilgrims to the Holy Land.
1095. Messr. Hickman and R Hood Wright.
1096. Sir John Buchanan-Jardine, Master of the Dumfriesshire Hounds.
1097. James Farrow.
1098. C A Phillips.
1099. Mrs Mary Amps.
1100. Major and Mrs Bell-Murray.
1101. Boughey family form Aqualate, Norfolk.
1102. The Clumber Spaniel was originally a French breed

developed by the Duc, who brought his kennels to Clumber Park, after he left France during the French Revolution.

1103. Gaston Pouchain, President of the French Kennel Club and the Brittany Spaniel Club of France.

1104. Cecil Moore.

1105. Earl of Malmesbury.

1106. Duke of Buccleuch.

1107. General Sir Douglas and Lady Brownrigg.

1108. William Arkwright.

1109. Duchess of Montrose.

1110. Newfoundland.

1111. 4 categories by colour: white, black, grey and yellow. Further divided by value and beauty.

1112. Physician in Chief to Queen Elizabeth I. Also co-founder of Caius College, Cambridge University.

1113. German Shorthaired Pointer.

1114. Captain John Edwards.

1115. Queen Victoria.

1116. Eurasier, or Eurasian dog.

1117. Irish Wolfhound, famous as a Red Cross dog during the 1st World War, who later shepherded sheep in Central Park, New York.

1118. Joseph Allen and Konrad Most.

1119. Harrison Weir.

1120. In 1894, J M Barrie married Mary Ansell, and on their honeymoon in Switzerland, they saw a litter of St Bernard puppies, and chose one.

1121. Gilbert White.

1122. R Lydekker.

1123. Konrad Lorenz.

1124. Major Herber.

1125. American Staffordshire Bull Terrier.

1126. Rodolphe Darzens.

1127. Mrs Raymond Mallock.

1128. King Henry IV's mistress, Corisande.

1129. Baron Freidrich von Steuben.

1130. Baron Georges Cuvier.

1131. King Henry VIII.

1132. King James I.
1133. Alexander Forbes of Aberdeen, 1617.
1134. Matthew Hopkins, the witchfinder general.
1135. Sir Edward Elgar.
1136. Sir Edward Elgar.
1137. All Base Section Commanders were to ensure that all pets at the army camps were not to be abandoned, and the Commanders were to liaise with the RSPCA.
1138. President of the FCI.
1139. Heinrich Essig.
1140. Robert Brooks.
1141. Charles Cruft.
1142. Lord Willoughby d'Eresly.
1143. Sir Everett Millais.
1144. Senator George Vest.
1145. Dr Rudolphina Menzel.
1146. Dr Henry Heimlich.
1147. Wing-Commander J A C and Mrs Ethnie Cecil-Wright.
1148. Group Captain "Beefy" and Mrs Catherine Sutton.
1149. J H Walsh.
1150. Rev. Thomas Pearce.
1151. Clifford Hubbard.
1152. Dr J Frank Perry.

Section 3

1153. Bijou.
1154. Greyfriars Bobby.
1155. Boatswain, Lord Byron's pet dog.
1156. Millie, George Bush's pet dog.
1157. Francis Redmond.
1158. Mrs W M Charlesworth.
1159. Sewallis E Shirley.
1160. Keeper, Emily and Charlotte Bronte's pet dog.
1161. Barry.
1162. Rin Tin Tin.
1163. Flush, Elizabeth Barratt Browning's pet dog.
1164. Lord Tweedmouth.
1165. Balthasar (John Galsworthy's Forsythe Saga).

1166. Rufus, Sir Winston Churchill's pet dog
1167. Snoopy

Section 4

1168. Basset Hound.
1169. Tibetan Terrier.
1170. Bullmastiff.
1171. Miniature Pinscher.
1172. Welsh Springer Spaniel.
1173. Soft Coated Wheaten Terrier.
1174. Pyrenean Mountain Dog.
1175. Pomeranian.
1176. Irish Setter.
1177. West Highland White Terrier.
1178. Airedale Terrier.
1179. Standard Poodle.
1180. St Bernard.
1181. French Bulldog.
1182. Japanese Chin.
1183. Hungarian Vizsla.
1184. Border Terrier.
1185. Borzoi.
1186. Minaiture Schnauzer.
1187. Smooth Collie.
1188. Lowchen.
1189. Kerry Blue Terrier.
1190. Lakeland Terrier.
1191. Dalmatian.
1192. Whippet.
1193. Cocker Spaniel (American).
1194. Boston Terrier.
1195. Old English Sheepdog.
1196. Bouvier de Flandres.
1197. Cocker Spaniel (American).
1198. Clumber Spaniel.
1199. Bulldog.
1200. Boxer.
1201. Greyhound.

Personalities Answers

1202. Akita.
1203. American Water Spaniel.
1204. American Wirehaired Pointing Griffon.
1205. Bloodhound.
1206. Borzoi.
1207. Brussels Griffon.
1208. Chesapeake Bay Retriever.
1209. Collie.
1210. Corgi (Cardigan Welsh).
1211. Chow Chow.
1212. Briard.
1213. Bernese Mountain Dog.
1214. Australian Terrier.
1215. Brittany.
1216. Chinese Crested Dog.
1217. Afghan Hound.

Arts Answers

Section 1

1218. Sir Arthur Conan Doyle.
1219. Homeward Bound.
1220. Shadow.
1221. Perdita.
1222. Old English Sheepdog.
1223. Rulf.
1224. Nana.
1225. Killing a rat.
1226. Hounds.
1227. W C Fields.
1228. Noel Coward.
1229. Toby.
1230. George, Lord Byron.
1231. Bullet (Trigger was his horse).
1232. The Flight of the Navigator.
1233. Howliday Inn.
1234. Rudyard Kipling.
1235. Oliver Goldsmith.
1236. Lewis Carroll.
1237. A black dog.
1238. Death, or the appearance of spirits.
1239. Kiss a dog.
1240. Lares and his dog.
1241. Aleuts.
1242. 3-headed guardian dog of Hades, who was dragged into the daylight by Hercules.
1243. A thief.
1244. Eric Knight.
1245. Italian Greyhound.
1246. Robinson Crusoe.
1247. Walt Disney cartoon extra-terrestrial dogs, possessing magical powers who end up on earth and have to pretend to be normal dogs until they are helped to return to their own planet.

1248. "Doggone" Valentine.
1249. Waggles.
1250. Bulldog.
1251. The Family dog, 1987.
1252. The Beagles.
1253. Spike, the Bulldog.
1254. Fox.
1255. Richard Adams.
1256. All dogs go to heaven (1989).
1257. The fox and the hound (1981).
1258. Silver Blaze, in the "Memoirs of Sherlock Holmes".
1259. Hounds.
1260. Talbot Hound.
1261. Hound on scent.
1262. Left the King's side, and attached itself to his enemy ,Henry of Lancaster.
1263. Hunting and hawking.
1264. Column of Marcus Aurelius.
1265. Hottest part of the summer (July-August) when Sirius, the dog star rises at dawn.
1266. St Bernard.
1267. Sir Percy Fitzpatrick.
1268. J F Herring.
1269. Weston Bell.
1270. 1970, coinciding with Expo '70 in Osaka.
1271. His Master's Voice.
1272. Toby, his Setter ate it.
1273. Hart to Hart.
1274. Napoleon.
1275. Patti Page.
1276. Diamond Dogs.
1277. Cat Stevens.
1278. Flanagan & Hall.
1279. Bonzo Dog Doo-Da Band.
1280. Snoop Doggy Dogg.
1281. Spike.
1282. Ralph.
1283. Old Mother Hubbard, by Sarah Catherine Martin.
1284. Troy.

1285. Newfoundland.
1286. John Galsworthy.
1287. Alexander Pope.
1288. Ogden Nash.
1289. George Bernard Shaw.
1290. Abbotsford.
1291. Ecclesiastes (IX, 4).
1292. Actaeon, the hunter.
1293. Dogs, horses and mules.
1294. Celestial dog of Chinese mythology.
1295. Pat.
1296. Laurel and Hardy's mongrel.
1297. Scraps.
1298. Dr Snuggles.
1299. Rude Dog and the Dweebs.
1300. Mississippi.
1301. No.
1302. Davey and Goliath.
1303. Translucent/invisible dog belonging to Jack Skellington, the Pumpkin King.
1304. Root Bolton.
1305. Tackhammer.
1306. Bob.
1307. Bob Carolgees.
1308. Jumble.
1309. Bruno.
1310. Mr Peabody.
1311. Scruffy.

Section 2

1312. John Heywood.
1313. Nathan Bailey.
1314. Mark Twain.
1315. Poodle.
1316. Airedale Terrier.
1317. Jean Cocteau.
1318. Sammy (short for Sampson), the Bull Terrier.
1319. Jerome K Jerome's Novel notes, 1893.

1320. Venerie de Jacques du Fouilloux, 1585.
1321. Dame Juliana Berners' "The Boke of St Albans", 1486.
1322. Thomas Brown's "Biographical sketches and authentic anecdotes of dogs, 1829.
1323. Thomas Carlye.
1324. Robert Scanlan's "My book of curs", 1840.
1325. Chapman Pincher.
1326. Baudelaire.
1327. Duke.
1328. P G Wodehouse's Jeeves.
1329. Emily Dickinson.
1330. Karel Capek.
1331. Dorothy Parker.
1332. John Steinbeck.
1333. To do what he wanted for one day, because all his life he had had to be good.
1334. Jeroslav Hasek's "The good soldier Svejk".
1335. Jack London's "The Call of the Wild".
1336. Samuel Pepys.
1337. Lord Macaulay.
1338. John Galsworthy's "The Silver Spoon" (part of the Forsythe Saga).
1339. Shoscombe Old Place.
1340. Strabo.
1341. War dogs, trained to fight in platoons, and used in the Roman army's front line.
1342. Greyhound.
1343. The Wife of Bath's prologue.
1344. Samuel Johnson.
1345. Caper (half Newfoundland, half Spaniel).
1346. George Elliot.
1347. John Dryden.
1348. Pug (Spectre of Tappington, Inglesby Legends).
1349. Elizabeth Barratt and Robert Browning.
1350. Miguel de Cervantes.
1351. Woodrow Wilson.
1352. The Merchant of Venice (Act 3, scene 3).
1353. Midsummer's Night Dream.
1354. Henry V (Act 2, scene 1).

1355. Henry IV Part 2 (Act 2, scene 4).

1356. Henry v (Act 3, scene 7).

1357. Julius Caesar Act 3, scene 1).

1358. Legend says that the Bishop Godfrey's hound deliberately ate a poisoned dish of food intended for his master.

1359. Saint Roche, patron saint of dogs, and whose protection is sought against rabies and the plague.

1360. Hounds were taken up to the church alter and fed cake. This provided protection against rabies throughout the year

1361. Keeping any greyhound or other dog for hunting.

1362. Wolves.

1363. Disrupted church services by barking, and sometimes tore up church books.

1364. Odysseus's dog, who still recognised his master when he returned in disguise after 19 years. Argus died from the joy of seeing Odysseus again.

1365. Pattern designed by the culture hero Maui, when he tattooed a dog's muzzle black.

1366. The cat wins the race by reaching home first, and so he is allowed to live indoors, while the dog must keep watch from outside.

1367. a. The dog helped Noah drive all the animals aboard the Ark and was the last animal to go aboard. There was no room for him inside, and so the dog spent 40 days with his nose in the rain.

b. The Ark sprang a leak, and the dog stopped the hole with his nose.

1368. Dogs were scavengers and ate the flesh of animals which were regarded as forbidden and unclean. Also associated with pagan idolatry.

1369. Family shaved themsleves as a symbol of deep mourning.

1370. Signalled the annual flooding of the Nile, and the need to move cattle to higher ground.

1371. Allbe, King Mesroda' of Leinster's hound.

1372. True.

1373. Anubis, the jackal-headed god of the death.

1374. Frighten away death. Also incarnation of the God Bhaironath.

1375. Their fingernails.

1376. Sicily.
1377. Reincarnated lamas punished for their faithlessness.
1378. Corpse-eating/pariah dogs.
1379. Kato Indians of California.
1380. Sent to the underworld to bring back the bones of the ancestors so that the first human pair could be created.
1381. Glen of Imaal Terrier.
1382. Pack of spectral hounds, often headless, and thought to be the spirits of unbaptised children, who roam through forests and woodland at night.
1383. Prince Rupert of the Rhine's poodle called Boye.
1384. Spectral hound said to haunt Peel Castle on the Isle of Man
1385. The 2-headed dog that guarded the red cattle of Geryon. Hercules's 10th task was to slay him.
1386. Alaunt.
1387. Simon de Monfort.
1388. Bloodhound and Scottish Terrier.
1389. Sir Edwin Landseer.
1390. Maud Earl.
1391. A hound.
1392. Sitting on the table next to the Duke.
1393. Relieving itself against one of the stable posts.
1394. Bonzo, by George Studdy.
1395. Alexandre-Francois Desportes.
1396. Thomas Gainsborough.
1397. Sir Edwin Landseer.
1398. French Bulldog, called Bouboule.
1399. Archie and Amos.
1400. Dog barking at the Moon.
1401. Max.
1402. Huckleberry Hound.
1403. True.
1404. Joseph Tabrar, sung by Miss Vesta Victoria.
1405. Most of Nimo's tricks were done without the handler being on the stage.
1406. Franklin D. Roosevelt (relating to his Scottish Terrier, Fala).
1407. The Dogfather, by Fritz Freling.
1408. Weakheart.

1409. Ralph Wolf and Sam Sheepdog
1410. Symbol of the devotion of dog in the service of man, commemorating the 1925 rescue sled drive 340 miles from Nenana to Nome. Diphtheria had broken out in Nome, and bad weather made transporting the medical serum immpossible apart from dog sled
1411. Early English period (c.1189-1307)

Section 3

1412. a. Samuel Pepys.
    b. King Charles II.
    c. Toy Spaniels (King Charles and Cavalier King Charles Spaniels).

1413. a. Montmorency.
    c. Jermone K Jerome.
    c. No.

1414. a. P G Wodehouse's character Uckridge.
    b. Training dogs for the music-hall stage.
    c. 6 Pekingese.

1415. a. Dr Watson does not know why he was sent to 3 Pinchin Lane, and just knows that he must get Toby!
    b. Sherlock Holmes.
    c. A mongrel. Half Spaniel, half lurcher which was used as a tracking dog to hunt for the murderers of Major Sholto.

1416. a. Part Bloodhound, part Mastiff.
    b. Bought from Ross and Mangles in Fulham, London.
    c. Island on Grimpen Mire.

1417. a. John Galsworthy in "The silver spoon" (Forsythe Saga).
    b. Dandie Dinmont and a Pekingese.
    c. Soames Forsyth.e

1418. a. John Galsworthy in "The Silver Spoon" (Forsythe Saga).

b. Dandie Dinmont.
c. Fleur Mont.

1419. a. Cecile Aubrey.
b. French Pyrenees.
c. Pyreneean Mountain Dog.

1420. a. Mr and Mrs Dearley.
b. Cruella De Vil, Jasper and Horace.
c. Make a fur coat out of the puppy skins.

1421. a. Dodie Smith.
b. The Starlight barking: more about the 101 Dalmatians.
c. Sirius, the Dog Star cast a spell over the whole world, and wanted to take all the dogs to be with him on the lonely star.

1422. a Alfred Bestall.
b. Pong-Ping, the Pekingese; Algy, the Pug.

1423. a. 12.
b. Live and let live.
c. Deceit deserves to be deceived.

1424. a. Woof.
b. Allan Ahlbery.
c. Norfolk Terrier.

1425. a. Fictional Liddesdale farmer in Sir Walter Scott's "Guy Mannering" who owned a special breed of terrier.
b. Mustard and Pepper according to their colour, with no other distinction apart from such adjectives as "Young", "Old" or "Little".
c. James Davidson of Hindlee.

1426. a. The New Yorker.
b. 1943.
c. "Is sex necessary", 1929. Written with E B White as co-author.

1427. a. George Elliot's "Middlemarch".
     b. St Bernard called Monk.

1428. a. Labes, tried for stealing a cheese.
     b. Alcibiades was an ancient Athenian General. Reputedly cut off his dog's tail in an attempt to distract the Athenians from his tyranny by such an act of eccentricity.
     c. Laelaps.

1429. a. I Kings 21:23.
     b. Matthew 15:27.
     c. The Song of Solomon 2:15.

1430. a. Florence Dombey – Dombey and Son.
     b. Mr Jingles – The Pickwick Papers.
     c. Dora Spenlow (later Copperfield) – David Copperfield.

1431. a. James Joyce's "Ulysses".
     b. G K Chesterton's "The Flying Inn".
     c. Charlotte Bronte's "Shirley".

1432. a. Ambrose Bierce "The enlarged devil's dictionary".
     b. Lilies in the field (Matthew 6:28).
     c. "Lowest rank in the hierarchy of dogs".

1433. a. Edward, 2nd Duke of York's manuscript "The master of game", 1406-13.
     b. Limited edition published in 1906.
     c. Sydenham Edward's Cynographia Britannica, 1800.

1434. a. W H Auden (In Memory of Sigmund Freud).
     b. Federico Garcia Lorca (Ballard of the Spanish Civil War).
     c. Ogden Nash (An Introduction to Dogs).

1435. a. Douglas Jerrold.
     b. William Penn.
     c. John B Bogart.

1436. a. Lion, dog and horse.

b. Scavenger dogs which ate corpses, and howled at the Moon.

c. Whelping bitch.

1437. a. Prince Llewellyn ap Joweth was out hunting, and returned to find his faithful hound Gelert covered in blood. His infant son's cradle was overturned and Llewellyn jumped to the conclusion that Gelert had attached and killed the baby. In his fury, he killed the dog, only to discover that Gelert had defended and killed a wolf that had attacked the baby, which was still alive.

b. Allegedly, King John gave the dog to Llewellyn.

c. Beddgelert, in Snowdonia.

1438. a. King Arthur's dog Cabal.

b. Cornwall.

c. Arthur's Troughs.

1439. a. Originally known as Culain, he was renamed Cuchulain after slaying the Great Smith of Ulster's watchdog. His name means Hound of Culain, and he was also known as the Hound of Ulster.

b. He could not eat dog flesh.

c. He took over the guarding duties of the watchdog he had killed.

1440. a. Odin, also known as Woden the Storm-God.

b. A spectral pack of hounds and huntsmen led by Woden who rode nightly in pursuit of a phantom boar, horse or woman.

c. A hound left on a hearth lived on ashes, howling and whining for a year.

1441. a. 7 swift hounds from Sparta.

b. The crowning of dogs with hawthorn to protect the dogs from the avenging spirits of wild animals they had killed.

c. Diana.

1442. a. The last sheaf.
      b. Killed the dog of the harvest.
      c. The Bitch.

1443. Cabilon, Lubina and Melampo.

1444. a. Guard-dog against stranger and burglars, but also
      protected the home against demons and evil spirits.
      b. A mosaic or painting of a chained dog, with the
      inscription "cave canem".
      c. Beware of the dog.

1445. a. Meissen.
      b. Rockingham.
      c. Royal Worcester.

1446. a. Weimaraner called Man Ray.
      b. Weimaraner called Fay Ray.

1447. a. William Hogarth.
      b. Trump.
      c. Tate Gallery, London.

1448. a. George Studd.y
      b. Yes.
      c. 1924.

1449. a. All of them.
      b. Yes.
      c. Friendship, protection and justice.

1450. a. Obelix.
      b. Dogmatix.
      c. Idefix.

1451. a. Asta.
      b. Schnauzer.
      c. Wirehaired Fox Terrier.

1452. a. Dorothy's dog in L Frank Braum's "The Wizard of Oz".
    b. Cairn Terrier.
    c. Border Terrier (Return to Oz).

1453. a. French Poodle.
    b. Bimbo the dog, and Ko-Ko the clown.

1454. a. Mark Twain's book "Roughing it", with its descriptions of coyotes and jackrabbits. Also Aesop's fable of the fox and the grapes.
    b. Always from the coyote's viewpoint.
    c. Never injures the roadrunner.

1455. a. Cartoon dog, who has ghost-hunting adventures.
    b. Great Dane.
    c. Scrappy-Doo.

1456. a. American Cocker spaniel.
    b. Jock.
    c. Blodhound.

1457. a. Glacier National Park, Montana, USA.
    b. New Mexico.
    c. King Edward III kenneled his greyhounds there.

1458. a. Pug.
    b. Her father, Lucian Freud.
    c. Trussardi.

1459. a. Petra, the Blue Peter dog.
    b. 1962.
    c. Shep, the Border Collie.

1460. a. Dogs and hunting.
    b. 2nd November.
    c. Against hunting injuries and rabies.

1461. a. The magic transformation of a man into a dog, or dog into the human form, or a form of insanity in which a person believes himself to be a dog.
   b. Transformation of human into wolf, or werewolves.

1462. a. War and peace.
   b. Siegfreid Sassoon.
   c. George Earl.

1463. a. Dogue de Bordeaux.
   b. German Shepherd Dog.
   c. Jack Russell Terrier.

1464. a. Shadow.
   b. Buster.
   c. Scamp.

1465. a. Eric Hill.
   b. Maurice Sendak.
   c. Afghan Hound.

1466. The height of a dog is measured from the ground to the withers (shoulder). See illustration below.
1467. The length of a dog is measured from the point of the shoulder to the point of the buttocks. See illustration below.

Feet

1468.	c.
1469.	b.
1470.	d.
1471.	a.

Profiles

1472.	a.
1473.	f.
1474.	c.
1475.	b.
1476.	e.
1477.	d.

Ears

1478.	d.
1479.	b.
1480.	c.
1481.	a.
1482.	f.
1483.	e.

Fronts

1484.	d.
1485.	a.
1486.	c.
1487.	f.
1488.	g.
1489.	e.
1490.	b.

Tails

1491.	c.
1492.	e.
1493.	f.
1494.	g.
1495.	a.
1496.	b.
1497.	j.
1498.	l.
1499.	i.
1500.	k.
1501.	h.
1502.	d.

QUESTION

"Where can I
buy the best
books
available on
my favourite
dog breeds?"